'**You're talking about Lord Birchenall's estate, aren't you?**' **She said it in a hoarse whisper while the blood drained from her face.** '**You're his son?**'

'That's right.' He studied her, his expression solemn. 'Does it matter?'

'I thought there was something about you—that I knew you from somewhere... I just never dreamt...' She pulled in a shaky breath and then looked up, her gaze meeting his. 'You've changed. You're so much more—' She broke off.

The gangly youth she remembered was gone. This man was muscled, toned, his features etched by the trials and tribulations of the years that had passed.

'I don't suppose you remember me?' He'd headed off to Medical School when she was around thirteen or fourteen years old. Why would he have given her a second thought?

'Of course I do.'

'Why didn't you tell me you knew who I was all along?' A flash of bitter defiance shot through her, making her green eyes spark with anger. 'You should have said something right from the start, when Zoe introduced us.'

'And lose the chance of talking to you?' His dark brows lifted. 'I may be many things, Ellie, but I'm not a fool.'

Dear Reader

I'm sure a lot of people have skeletons in their cupboards, scandals that affect their families, or things they might have done long ago that they regret when they're a bit older and wiser.

And that set me to wondering... What would happen if my heroine's former indiscretions came back to haunt her? And how would she cope if those transgressions promised to ruin her career and maybe destroy her chance of happiness with the man she loves?

Well, to find out what happens you'll need to read all about Ellie and James and their troubled path to true love.

Happy reading!

Joanna

SHELTERED BY HER TOP-NOTCH BOSS

BY
JOANNA NEIL

MILLS & BOON®

First published in Great Britain 2013
by Mills & Boon, an imprint of Harlequin (UK) Limited,
Large Print edition 2014
Eton House, 18-24 Paradise Road,
Richmond, Surrey, TW9 1SR

© 2013 Joanna Neil

ISBN: 978 0 263 23862 4

Harlequin (UK) Limited's policy is to use papers that are natural, renewable and recyclable products and made from wood grown in sustainable forests. The logging and manufacturing processes conform to the legal environmental regulations of the country of origin.

Printed and bound in Great Britain
by CPI Antony Rowe, Chippenham, Wiltshire

When **Joanna Neil** discovered Mills & Boon®, her lifelong addiction to reading crystallised into an exciting new career writing Mills & Boon® Medical Romance™. Her characters are probably the outcome of her varied lifestyle, which includes working as a clerk, typist, nurse and infant teacher. She enjoys dressmaking and cooking at her Leicestershire home. Her family includes a husband, son and daughter, an exuberant yellow Labrador and two slightly crazed cockatiels. She currently works with a team of tutors at her local education centre, to provide creative writing workshops for people interested in exploring their own writing ambitions.

Recent titles by Joanna Neil:

RETURN OF THE REBEL DOCTOR
HIS BRIDE IN PARADISE
TAMED BY HER BROODING BOSS
DR RIGHT ALL ALONG
DR LANGLEY: PROTECTOR OR PLAYBOY?
A COTSWOLD CHRISTMAS BRIDE
THE TAMING OF DR ALEX DRAYCOTT
BECOMING DR BELLINI'S BRIDE

These books are also available in eBook format from www.millsandboon.co.uk

CHAPTER ONE

ELLIE SHIFTED RESTLESSLY on the barstool, crossing one long, elegant leg over the other. How much longer would it be before she could decently slip away from here? She cradled a cocktail glass between her fingers and watched her friends enjoying themselves. She was the only one out of kilter here.

The party was in full swing, the heavy beat of music drowning out the buzz of conversation, though every now and again a burst of laughter broke through the din. Some people were on the dance floor, and everyone seemed contented, eager to let their hair down.

If only she could feel the same way. She'd had an awful day, though, and she desperately wanted it to end. This was the last place she needed to be.

'I'm glad you managed to get here tonight after all,' Lewis said, moving closer. 'I know you had to work late today.' His hazel eyes were warm as he gazed at her. An errant lock of brown, wavy hair fell across his forehead.

She nodded and made an effort to put on a cheerful expression. But how much more small talk could she make? She'd spent the last hour doing that, and all the while she'd been hoping for the chance to say goodbye and leave the party relatively unnoticed, some time soon.

'I had to try,' she said. 'I know how keen Zoe was to have us all come to her celebration.' She smiled, seeing her friend circle the room, chatting to people who'd been her colleagues for the last few years. 'I'll miss her, but I'm glad she managed to get the promotion she wanted. It's just sad that she'll be moving away from here.'

'Well, she's only going as far as the next county—I dare say she'll be coming back to Cheshire to visit us every now and again.'

'Yes, I suppose you're right.' She drained the

last of her drink and then said, 'I haven't seen your wife here tonight. Couldn't she make it?'

Lewis shook his head and looked uncomfortable. 'She…uh…had to go to another do. A family thing.' His voice trailed off, and just as Ellie was absorbing that, Zoe came over to them.

Ellie's eyes widened a fraction as she glanced at the man who accompanied her. His brooding gaze wandered over her in turn, and there was something about him that caused a frisson of awareness to shiver down her spine. Did she know him from somewhere? Snatches of memory flickered through her mind and dissolved as fast as they had come into being.

But how could she have forgotten him? He was tall, and exceptionally good-looking, wearing an immaculate dark suit. Peeping out from beneath his jacket sleeves, the cuffs of his shirt were pristine, fastened with stylish gold cuff links. But the feeling remained, niggling at the outer edges of her consciousness. She felt strangely uneasy.

'Ellie, I must introduce you to James,' Zoe said, bubbling with enthusiasm, her blonde hair quivering with every small movement she made. 'He's taking over from me at the hospital—honestly, I'm already regretting taking the new job. Would you credit it? Just as I'm leaving, *he* turns up?' She rolled her eyes in an *'Isn't he to die for?'* kind of way, and James laughed, a soft, rumbling sound coming from the back of his throat.

He looked at Ellie, appreciation sparking in his smoke-grey eyes before he tilted his head in acknowledgement to Lewis.

'It's good to meet you, Ellie,' James said, his voice a deep, satisfying murmur that whispered along her nerve endings and turned her insides to jelly.

'Likewise.'

'I understand you work with Lewis?'

She nodded. 'We're in different departments, but we're both at the hospital. I'm a registrar in A and E.'

Ellie studied him from under her lashes. She could see what Zoe meant. He had the kind of looks that had her stomach doing peculiar flips, despite her initial misgivings about him, while her senses were falling over each other as they clamoured for attention.

He *was* gorgeous, there was no doubt about it. He had black hair, beautiful grey eyes and perfectly proportioned, angular features, along with a body that was lithe and muscular, radiating energy. Even in her present unhappy state of mind she managed to register all those things.

James turned to Lewis. 'Hi,' he said. 'Are you and Jessica still coming over to the house this weekend?'

'Yes, we are.'

'Good. We'll look forward to seeing you there.'

Lewis nodded. 'James is my cousin,' he explained to Ellie. 'He's always taken it on himself to watch out for me. I lost my parents when I was in my teens, you see, and his father took me in.'

'Ah, I see.' She hesitated. 'I'm sorry to hear about your parents, I never knew that. I guess there must be a strong bond between you and your cousin because of that—you're a bit like brothers, I suppose?'

'That's right.'

'I make sure he stays on the straight and nar-row,' James said with a smile. 'Though I've been away for a while and perhaps I need to catch up with the latest news. I'd no idea he was working with such a beautiful woman.'

Seeing their absorption with one another, Zoe gave a satisfied smile and walked away from them, taking a reluctant Lewis along with her. 'I want you to meet a friend of mine,' she told him.

Ellie set her empty glass down on the bar and glanced at James. 'I thought I caught a glimpse of you earlier,' she murmured. Even then, she'd been on edge without knowing why. Perhaps it was all down to the horrible day she'd had.

He smiled. 'Same here. I saw you come over to the bar a few minutes ago. The truth is,' he confided, 'I've been badgering Zoe to introduce us ever since.' His glance wandered over her, drifting down over the dress that clung where it touched, over her long, silk-clad legs, still crossed at the knee, and came back up to linger on the mass of burnished chestnut curls that lightly brushed her shoulders.

Her skin heated as though it had been licked by flame. No man had ever had this effect on her, turning her body to fire with a single glance.

She struggled to get control of herself, and then looked at him once more. Perhaps she knew him from seeing him around the hospital?

'I heard you've already started working in A and E,' she said, 'but I don't think we've actually met before this, have we? Somehow, I had the feeling…' She added quickly, 'It gets so busy in the emergency unit, I don't always have the opportunity to meet up with new people straight away.'

'I've been working the night shift,' he answered, 'getting to know the lie of the land. Officially, my job as consultant doesn't start for a couple of days.' He studied her once more. 'I feel I do know you already, though. I often watch your TV programme—*Your Good Health*.' He gave her a crooked smile, and there was a mischievous glint in his eye.

'I have to tell you, you're my very favourite TV presenter—you look terrific both on and off camera, and you make medicine seem like child's play. I imagine every red-blooded male who watches the programme secretly yearns for you to be there to mop his brow.'

She laughed. 'I very much doubt that, but thank you anyway. I enjoy doing the show. It makes a change from A and E and I hope I might be doing some good, maybe helping people to look after themselves.'

'I'm sure what you do is extremely useful.' He looked at her empty glass. 'Can I get you a refill?'

She shook her head. 'Actually, I was just about to leave. It's been a long day, one way and another. I think I'll ring for a taxi.'

'You're not enjoying the party?' He frowned. 'I wondered if there was something amiss when I saw you earlier. You seemed preoccupied, a little despondent maybe? Is it something you want to talk about?'

'Not really.' She eased herself off the barstool, pulling down the hem of her dress and smoothing the material over her hips. His gaze followed the movement of her hands and she said huskily, 'There's no reason for me to spoil your evening by involving you in my problems. I've had a difficult day and I should never have come here, but I didn't want to let Zoe down.'

'I understand.' He frowned. 'I'm sorry you're feeling that way. Maybe I could see you home? I have my car outside. Whereabouts do you live?'

'Ashleigh Meadows, but I don't want to put you out. I'll be fine, really. You should stay and enjoy the party.'

'That's okay. It's no trouble. I didn't intend to stay long anyway.' He glanced at the gold watch on his wrist. 'I have to be on duty at the hospital in just over an hour, and Ashleigh Meadows is on my way.'

'Oh, I see.' She hesitated. It wouldn't hurt to accept his offer, would it? 'Well, in that case, okay. Thanks.' She glanced quickly around the room. 'I'd better take a minute to go and say goodbye to Zoe.'

He nodded and went with her, and a few min-

utes later they were both sitting in his luxuri-
ously upholstered car, with the air-conditioning
switched on and soft music coming from the CD
player. She gave him directions to her house, and
after driving for a few minutes James turned
the car onto the Ashleigh Road. Ellie sat back,
lulled by the soft purr of the engine, trying to
relax and let the music soothe her battered soul.

James slanted her an oblique look. 'Are you
sure you don't want to tell me about it? Whatever it was, it seems to have made a powerful
impact on you. Was it personal or something
that happened in A and E?'

Her first instinct was to stay closed up and
keep things to herself. She certainly wasn't going
to tell him her worries about her brother and his
constant battle with debt. Noah had phoned her
first thing that morning, worried about the way
things were going with his finances. She loved
her younger brother and would do anything she
could to help him out, but his situation troubled
her.

But as to the other problem—what was the

point in keeping it to herself after all? No one could make it better, but perhaps talking it over with a colleague might help her to come to terms with what happened.

She gave a shuddery sigh. 'A patient died,' she told him. 'I know it happens from time to time, and as doctors we should be able to deal with it, but this was someone I knew—the aunt of an old schoolfriend of mine. I knew her quite well and it was such a terrible shock when she died. It was upsetting that I couldn't save her. I kept asking myself if I did everything possible.'

His brow creased in sympathy. 'I'm sorry. It must have been terrible for you to go through that, especially with someone you knew.' He turned off the main road and the car's headlights picked out the country lane, stretched out like a ribbon before them, throwing the overgrown hedgerows on either side into deep shadow.

She nodded. 'But it was worse for Amelia. Her aunt virtually brought her up, and she was dev-astated when she died.' She hesitated, her voice dropping to a hoarse whisper. 'She blames me for letting it happen.'

He exhaled sharply. 'You mustn't take it to heart. It's the shock—sometimes people just can't accept it when a loved one dies. They say and do things while they're emotionally upset and often come to regret it afterwards. I'm sure you did everything you could for your friend's aunt.'

Ellie winced. 'I'm afraid Mel doesn't see it that way. Perhaps if she knew me better she might have more confidence in me, but we lost touch after we left school and moved in different circles.' She frowned, thinking back over what had happened. 'She thinks I should have changed her aunt's medication and sent her for surgery, but I'm not sure if there was anything I could have done to change the outcome.'

'What was wrong with her aunt?' He slowed the car as a cluster of houses came into view, yellow points of light illuminating the village in the darkness.

'There was an inflammation around her heart.

She was brought to A and E in a state of collapse, with severe chest pain and breathlessness. I put her on oxygen and monitored her vital signs, did blood tests and sent her for a CT scan, as well as echocardiography.' She sucked in a breath.

'The tests showed that she had an acute bacterial infection that had caused the pericardium to become congested with purulent matter. I put her on strong antibiotics and started to drain the pericardial fluid, but in the end her heart simply stopped.' Her voice choked. 'I think her age and general frailty worked against her. Her heart couldn't take the strain.'

'And you explained all that to your friend?'

She nodded. 'Yes, but I don't know whether she took it all in. I fetched her a cup of tea and sat with her for a while, and tried to explain, but it was as though she was frozen. She seemed not to hear what I said. She was upset and angry at the same time.'

He pressed his lips together in a grim line. 'It happens that way sometimes.'

'I suppose so.' She looked out of the window as the cottages drew near. 'Mine's the old farmhouse,' she told him. 'Turn next left, and it's at the end of the track.'

A short time later he pulled the car up on the gravelled drive outside the brick-built house. A lantern in the wide, slate-roofed porch gave off a welcoming glow, highlighting the ivy-covered walls and the tidy front garden.

'Judging from what I can see by the light of the moon, you have a very attractive place here,' James commented.

Ellie nodded. 'I'm glad you like it. I'd had my eye on it for a while, and when it came on the market I jumped at the chance to buy.' She gave a wry smile. 'It needed a lot of renovation, so at least it was within my budget. I like it because it's not crowded out by other properties—there's just the converted barn across the courtyard at the back of the house.'

She paused then asked hesitantly, 'Do you have time to come in for a coffee before your shift starts? I could give you a quick look inside, if you like.' She'd only just met him, but he had a warm and sympathetic manner, and she wanted to be with him just a little bit longer.

'That would be great, thanks. I like these old farmhouse cottages—they have a lot of character.'

'That's how I feel, too.' She slid out of the car, leaving its comforting warmth for the coolness of the summer evening, and together they walked to the front door. 'Though cottage is perhaps a bit of a misnomer—it's quite cosy inside, but there are two storeys.'

The door opened into a large entrance hall, and she led the way from there to the kitchen, where James admired the golden oak beams and matching oak units.

'This was the first room I renovated,' she said, spooning freshly ground coffee into the percolator. 'The beams were dark with age, so I had them cleaned up and then picked out cupboards to go with the new, lighter colour.'

James nodded. 'They make the room look warm and homely.' His gaze went to the gleaming range cooker that she'd lovingly restored and which had pride of place in her kitchen. 'That must help heat up the kitchen.'

She nodded. 'It does. I love it—I spend lots of time experimenting with new recipes—it's kind of a hobby. Cooking helps me to unwind.' She smiled. 'Though I live here on my own, so I often have to share what I've made with the family across the way...the people who live in the converted barn.'

He looked her over, amusement sparking in his eyes, and once again she experienced that odd feeling of familiarity, as though she knew him from somewhere in the past, but once again the circumstances eluded her.

'You cook as well?' he said. 'Wow. Fortune's following me around today—I must have stumbled on my dream woman!'

She chuckled. 'I wouldn't get too carried away, if I were you—I didn't say I was any good at it.'

He laughed, and while the percolator simmered, she showed him the living/dining room that was tacked on to one end of the open plan kitchen. 'I had the wall taken down,' she said, 'to make the place seem bigger. I was a bit worried it might not work out too well.'

'I don't think that's a problem at all.' He stood close to her as they surveyed the room, and all she could think about was his nearness, the long line of his strong and lean body, the way his arm inadvertently brushed hers and sent a ripple of heat surging inside her.

He glanced at her, and there was a stillness about him that made her wonder if he'd experienced that same feeling. He seemed distracted for a moment or two and then appeared to force his attention back to the subject in hand.

'It all seems to work pretty well. The dining area goes on from the kitchen, and the living room is part of the L-shape, which makes it kind of separate. All the rooms benefit from the extra space.'

She nodded, struggling to regain control of herself. 'That's what I was hoping for. There's a small utility room as well, so I have just about everything I need here. I'm really fortunate to have this place, but it's the extra money from the TV show that funded all the renovations.'

'I can imagine.' His mouth made a crooked line. 'But as an avid fan, I'm convinced you're worth every penny they pay you. You explain things in a way people can understand, and make the programme lively and interesting at the same time.'

'I'm glad you think so, but it's all down to teamwork really. It doesn't take too long to make the programmes, so it's worked out pretty well for me, all in all.' She sent him a quizzical glance. 'Perhaps it's something you'd like to try? The producers are always looking for new presenters.'

He shook his head. 'I don't think so. I'm busy enough as it is. I've enough going on outside medicine to keep me occupied. So time out for a spot of rest and relaxation would be first on my agenda, and I like to spend it on my boat, where I can get away from everything and everyone.' He sent her an oblique glance, his mouth making a teasing curve. 'Is there any chance you might want to join me? I could set aside a few days especially for you and we could maybe spend a long, lazy weekend together.'

She gave him an answering smile. 'That's a tempting proposition, James, but I'd really have to give it some thought.' It had definite appeal, but some innate sense made her hold back.

She'd been in relationships before, which had promised so much and then proved to be a huge letdown. Perhaps her background, the disintegration of her family life had made her cautious about expecting too much. 'We barely know each other, after all.'

'That could soon be remedied.'

They walked back to the kitchen, and Ellie poured coffee, smiling faintly as the tempting aroma teased her nostrils. Despite her reservations, she liked being with James. She'd been feeling thoroughly down in the dumps and somehow he'd managed to pull her out of the swamp of depression.

She handed him a cup and he added cream and sugar, stirring thoughtfully. 'So how did you get into the TV business?' he asked, as they sipped the hot liquid. 'Were you spotted by a talent scout prowling the emergency unit?'

She laughed. 'No such luck. I know someone who works at the studios, and she suggested I might like to try it. I'd written a few articles for magazines and made a couple of videos for students that turned out all right, so she thought I might take to it.'

'And I guess she was right.'

'Mmm, it seems so.' She rummaged in the fridge and the cupboard, looking for something to nibble on. 'Would you like something to eat? Biscuits and cheese, or a slice of quiche maybe?'

He shook his head and took a quick sip of coffee. 'Not for me, thanks,' he said, and there was a hint of resignation in his tone. 'I'm afraid I must be going very soon.'

'Oh, of course. Okay.' She felt a pang of disappointment because he was about to leave. They drank their coffees and talked about her TV work for a while longer. Then he put down his cup and started to head towards the door.

'You said you lead a busy life,' she murmured as she walked with him. 'What is it that takes up most of your time outside work?'

'I help to manage my father's estate. The manager has taken extended leave to deal with a family crisis in Ireland, so I've had to step into the breach in the meantime.'

His father's estate. She frowned, and all at once alarm bells started to ring faintly inside her head. Memories of her past came flooding back to haunt her, causing a feeling of nausea to start up in her stomach, and she tried to quash the thoughts that were crowding her mind. There wasn't necessarily anything untoward in what he was saying.

'His estate?' she said in a guarded voice. 'That sounds like something quite involved. What kind of estate is it?'

'Farming, mostly, with a dairy and creamery on site. There are other things going on there as well—there's an orchard, and a lake where people can go to fish.' He glanced at her, as though gauging her reaction. 'My father isn't too well at the moment, so he's finding it difficult to oversee things. He tried to get someone to take over the management on a temporary basis, but that hasn't worked out so I've had to get involved.'

'You're talking about Lord Birchenall's estate, aren't you?' She said it in a hoarse whisper, while the blood drained from her face. 'You're his son?'

'That's right.' He studied her, his expression solemn. 'Does it matter?'

'I thought there was something about you—that I knew you from somewhere. I just never dreamt...' She pulled in a shaky breath and then looked up, her gaze meeting his. 'You've changed. You're so much more...' She broke off. The gangly youth she remembered was gone.

This man was muscled, toned, his features etched by the trials and tribulations of the years that had passed. 'I don't suppose you remember me?' He'd headed off to medical school when she had been around thirteen or fourteen years old. Why would he have given her a second thought?

'Of course I do. It was a long while ago, and you've filled out in all the right places, but how could I forget you, Ellie? You were always up to something, climbing trees, camping out in the woods. I watched out for you, in case you landed yourself in a scrape.'

He'd watched out for her? She cast that thought to one side. 'Why didn't you tell me you knew who I was all along?' A flash of bitter defiance shot through her, making her green eyes spark with anger. 'You should have said something right at the start, when Zoe introduced us.'

'And lose the chance of talking to you?' His dark brows lifted. 'I may be many things, Ellie, but I'm not a fool.'

'No, you're Lord Birchenall's son—and you've been brought up to believe in his values and everything he stands for.'

'And what would those be, Ellie?'

'That all that matters is his own comfort, his own perfectly organised way of life.' She bit out the words through clenched teeth as she gave vent to her feelings of resentment and betrayal. 'Nothing must get in the way of his wellbeing, must it? Woe betide any hapless worker who falls foul of Lord Birchenall.'

'Aren't you being a little melodramatic?'

She gasped. 'How can you say that to me? My father was Lord Birchenall's estate manager for a dozen or more years until your father sacked him and threw him off his land. We lost everything…the house that went with the job, our livelihood, our unity as a family.'

'I know that must have been a tremendous blow to you, but are you so sure your father didn't bring it on himself? I remember my father being angry, at the end of his tether. Things had not been running smoothly, there were glitches, problems. I don't know all the reasons why it happened, Ellie, but I'm sure my father wouldn't have acted without due cause.'

'And you didn't care what became of his family afterwards?'

'That's not true. I did care. But I went away

to medical school around about that time, and I didn't know what went on after I left. I asked my father what happened to you and he said you'd moved to a house in the village.'

She opened the front door and stood to one side to let him pass.

'What else could we do? We had to move in with friends for the first few months. He ruined our lives, that's what happened.' She pressed her lips together to hold back the anger that was taking hold of her. 'I'd hoped I could put it behind me after all these years, but now it's come flooding back with a vengeance.'

She stiffened, bracing her shoulders, and her gaze locked with his. 'You should go,' she said.

He stepped outside into the porch, and then turned to face her once more. 'I'm sorry you feel this way. It was all a long time ago. Maybe it's time for you to let it go.'

'I don't think that's possible.'

'That's unfortunate.' He frowned, studying her face in the moonlight. 'Goodnight, Ellie.' He

nodded briefly and then strode across the gravelled drive to his car.

She watched him go. She'd thought the day
couldn't get any worse…

CHAPTER TWO

'THANKS FOR THIS, Ellie.' Noah folded the cheque Ellie had given him and slid it into his wallet. 'I'll pay you back as soon as I can, I promise.'

Her brother looked earnest, his youthful features lit with relief. 'It's just that things are difficult for me right now, with the magazine closing down—it was my best source of income. But I'll make a go of this freelance work, I know I will.'

'I'm sure you will, eventually.' Ellie finished off the last slice of toast and brushed the crumbs from her fingers. It was worrying, the way things had been going for him lately. They'd been through a lot together, and she'd always looked out for him. If only there was some way she could help him get out of this mess.

'Perhaps you could look for something a bit more secure in the meantime? There must be some regular jobs in photography—in advertising, maybe, or even something like illustrating medical books. I know it's not what you're used to.'

He pulled a face, his hazel eyes troubled. 'I'll try, honestly I will—I know I need to sort something out. I've spent the whole weekend looking for alternatives. But photojournalism's what I'm really interested in.'

She nodded, and began to clear away the breakfast dishes. 'Did you want any more tea, or shall I empty the pot?'

'I'm fine, thanks. I should go and try to appease the landlord.' He patted the wallet in his pocket. 'This will keep him off my back for a while at least.'

'And I must get ready for work.' Her green eyes clouded momentarily and Noah gave her a thoughtful look. 'Is something wrong? You don't look too happy about that. I thought you loved your work?'

'I do…mostly.' Her patient's death still haunted her, and the whole episode with Mel's unsettling reaction had thrown her off balance somehow. It would take her some time to get back into her stride.

But that wasn't it.

'The new consultant's starting work today.' She winced. 'I met him at Zoe's party—turns out he's Lord Birchenall's son.'

'Birchenall?' Noah bit out the word with distaste. 'No wonder you're out of sorts. I thought we'd seen the last of that family.' He frowned. 'Perhaps I should have guessed. I read in the paper that he was back home to take care of his father—the old man is suffering from some kind of heart condition, apparently.'

'Is he? James said he was unwell, but he didn't go into detail.'

'James? You're on first-name terms with him?' Noah's lips tightened. 'I wish you didn't have to deal with him at all. How do we know it won't turn out to be like father, like son? You could go along with him thinking everything's fine, and then when something goes wrong you find he's turned against you. It's all in the genes.'

'You could be right,' she acknowledged thoughtfully. 'We'll see. I suppose I'll just have to be cautious around him until I get to know him better.'

'Yeah, well, it's a pity you have to know him at all. I'm sorry you've ended up having to work with him.' He frowned. 'I'd better go. Thanks for breakfast, and good luck.'

'You, too.'

After he'd gone, Ellie finished tidying the kitchen and glanced at the clock on the wall. It was about time for her to set off for work, but just as she reached for her jacket, the doorbell rang.

'Lily.' Ellie was startled to see her neighbour standing there. Lily was heavily pregnant, and right now she looked flushed and her breathing was fast, making her struggle to drag air into her lungs. Her face appeared a little puffy, and when Ellie glanced down at her hands, she saw that there was some swelling there, too. Her brown curls were faintly damp around her face, and Ellie became increasingly concerned. 'Are you all right? Is it the baby? Are you having contractions?'

Lily shook her head. 'No, but I have to go to hospital—the ambulance will be here any minute. The midwife sent for it. I have a terrible headache, and my ankles are swollen. She said something about hypertension and pre-eclampsia—she thinks they'll keep me in for a few days.'

'I'm so sorry, Lily.' Ellie put a comforting arm around her. 'Do you want to sit down? Shall I get you a chair?'

Lily shook her head. 'No, thanks. But I do need to ask a big favour.' She gave her a worried look.

'It's okay. Anything. What is it? What can I do for you?'

'It's Jayden—he's at nursery school right now, and my friend will pick him up and look after him after school, but I wondered, just in case they do keep me in, if you would have him stay with you for the next few nights? I know it's an awful lot to ask, but Harry's away in Switzerland, trying to sort out some problems with the company, and my parents are on holiday abroad. I don't know what else to do.'

Ellie thought about the small guest bedroom upstairs. She'd have to bump up the heating in there and get in a few provisions to satisfy a four-year-old's diet, but otherwise there shouldn't be a problem. 'That's okay. I can do that for you. I'll be glad to help. And Jayden often comes here to see me, so he's used to being around the place. Don't worry about it. Just concentrate on getting yourself well again.'

'Oh, thanks, Ellie,' Lily said in a relieved tone. 'I don't know what I'd have done without you. Here, have my key—you'll need to pick up some clothes for Jayden and some of his toys.' An anxious look crossed her face. 'He always takes his teddy to bed with him. He won't sleep without it.'

'I'll make sure he has it. Rest easy, and take care of yourself.'

The midwife came to help Lily back to her house across the courtyard as the ambulance arrived, and Ellie went with them, waving her neighbour goodbye before setting off for the hospital. It was worrying, seeing her in that situation, but at least the paramedics were with her and would take care of her.

The A and E department was busy as usual when she arrived there a short time later. She'd had a weekend away from work and she found she was apprehensive coming back to it, a little bit uneasy about dealing with patients who were very ill, after her experience with her friend's aunt. Although she felt she'd followed the correct procedures, her confidence had been badly shaken by Mel's outburst. It was difficult getting back into the fray, but after an hour or so she had more or less settled into the routine and her anxiety eased a little.

From time to time she caught sight of James, working with the most seriously ill patients, and she did her very best to steer clear of him. In a way she was regretting her outburst the other night, because he hadn't done anything to deserve her wrath. It was just his family connection that had thrown her into a state of shock.

But she had to put all that aside if she was to do her job properly. Just now she was tending a young woman who'd fallen from a horse. Until the accident the girl had been enjoying a holiday at a pretty lakeside resort nearby, but her fall meant she'd ended up in the emergency unit, being treated for a broken arm.

'That was unfortunate, wasn't it, Natalie?' Ellie murmured. 'But the good news is that the X-ray shows a straightforward break. We'll realign the bones for you under anaesthetic and then immobilise them with a cast. We should soon have you feeling more comfortable.'

'Thanks.' Natalie pulled a face. 'I guess that's put an end to my horse riding for a while.'

'I'm afraid so. It'll probably take six or eight weeks to heal, and you should be careful with it in the meantime. So...' she smiled '...I'd avoid abseiling or waterskiing for the time being.'

The girl laughed. 'I'll bear that in mind.'

Ellie left her with a nurse while she went to

type up her notes on the computer. After a moment or two as she sat at the desk, she became aware of someone approaching, and looked up to see James coming to stand beside her. Her whole body tensed.

He was immaculately turned out, having discarded the scrubs he'd been wearing earlier and replaced them with a dark, expertly tailored suit and a crisp linen shirt that gave him an aura of authority. He wore a subtly patterned tie that picked out the colour of his smoke-grey eyes.

Maybe he was dressed this way because he had a meeting to attend. Either way, Ellie found his nearness extremely distracting. It unsettled her. She didn't want to be aware of him, especially not as a virile, energetic and powerful man.

'How are things going?' he asked. His expression was serious, his eyes cool and watchful. 'Are you getting back into the swing of things? I know it must have been difficult for you. I noticed you were a little hesitant at first when you were dealing with patients.'

Her eyes widened. Had he feared she wouldn't be able to cope? She stiffened.

'I'm fine,' she answered. 'There's no problem, none at all.'

'Hmm. You must tell me if things change.' He looked doubtful, and she guessed he thought she was covering up. 'After all, it's my job to see to the welfare of the staff, as well as the patients. I don't want you to feel that you must struggle on your own.'

'As I said, I don't foresee any difficulties.' If she'd known who he was the other night, she would never have admitted her worries to him. It had been a bad mistake. No doubt from now on he'd be watching her like a hawk.

She turned her attention back to the screen in front of her. With any luck, he might take the hint and leave her to get on with her work.

But things definitely weren't going her way. Instead, he sat down on the edge of the table and out of the corner of her eye she caught a glimpse of his long legs, the material of his trousers stretched tautly over his strong thighs. Disconcerted, she quickly averted her gaze.

Her fingers tapped jerkily at the keypad, and she realised straight away she'd made mistakes so that she had to delete what she'd just typed.

'Um, was there something else?' she queried. Having him so close jangled her nerves.

He inclined his head. 'I think you and I have some unfinished business,' he said quietly. 'I know you feel a lot of resentment towards me and my family, and I'm concerned that might be a problem for us at work.'

'I...I'm sure we can both act in a professional manner towards one another,' she said. 'Perhaps I was wrong in extending your father's actions to you, but I can't simply forget what happened, as you suggested. My parents' marriage fell apart because of it. My mother blamed my father for losing his job and making us all homeless.'

'Your mother felt that way, and yet you still put the blame on my father for letting him go?' His gaze was quizzical, those dark eyes studying her and taking in the slightest hint of vulnerability.

Her chin lifted in defiance. 'I think there were reasons why my father acted the way he did. He's a good man, and he always took a lot of pride in doing his job well. When things started to go wrong, your father should have talked to him a bit more and tried to get to the bottom of what was going on with him.'

James was sceptical. 'It doesn't seem as if your mother had much faith in her husband, so why should my father have been any different?'

Her eyes narrowed. 'My mother suffered from depression. She was always a difficult person to live with. She was so wrapped up in her woes that she left me and my brother to fend for ourselves. We took care of one another, and did pretty much as we pleased, but through all that my father was the cement that kept us all together. That is, until he...'

'Until he lost the plot.' He stood up. 'I'm sorry, Ellie. I know how much you must love him, but you're making excuses for his behaviour and taking your resentment out on my family. You need to get things straightened out in your head.'

'Do I?' Her gaze was frosty. 'I believe my father was ill. That's why he appeared to change and became lax in his work where before he had been a perfectionist. But nobody seemed to care enough about him to find out what was going on.'

She stood up as her pager bleeped. 'I'm afraid you'll have to excuse me. I have a patient coming in.'

She was annoyed with herself as she walked away. How could she have lost her temper that way? Surely she could have handled things better? And now, instead of smoothing the way towards a better working relationship, she'd probably set them off on a course of downright antagonism.

She had to force that to the back of her mind, though, and concentrate on answering her pager. She couldn't let her personal life interfere with her work.

Her patient was a pregnant woman who was bleeding heavily. 'She was out shopping when she collapsed,' the nurse told her. 'She's very shaken up. She's thirty-three weeks. Her heart rate is very fast and her blood pressure's dropping way too low.'

'Thanks, Olivia. Let's get a couple of intravenous lines in before she goes into shock—and we need to set up foetal monitoring.'

'I'll do that right away.' The nurse hurried to fetch the equipment while Ellie did an ultrasound scan to find out what was causing the problem. 'I know this is upsetting for you, Phoebe,' she said gently, 'but try not to worry.'

Phoebe nodded faintly. Small pearls of perspiration had broken out on her brow, dampening her dark hair, and Ellie gave her a reassuring smile. 'We'll take good care of you and your baby.'

A short time later, she turned to the nurse once more. 'I'm going to call Dr Reynolds for a consultation,' she said in a low voice. 'The placenta's covering the birth canal. It's come away slightly, and that's what's causing the bleeding. We need to admit her and make sure that she rests—that way the bleeding might stop on its own.'

She began to take blood for testing and quickly labelled up the samples for the lab. She was handing them to a porter a few minutes later when Lewis came to join her.

He smiled. 'Hi, Ellie. It's good to see you. You have a patient for me?'

'Yes.' She returned his smile. 'I'm glad you're here, Lewis. It's reassuring to know you're around to look after our pregnant ladies.' She handed him the patient's file. 'Phoebe has placenta praevia. I've arranged for her to be admitted.'

He glanced at the woman's notes. 'Okay, I'll go and have a look at her.'

He came back to Ellie a few minutes later as she stood by the central desk glancing through reports.

'We might have to do a Caesarean,' he said, 'but I'd prefer to leave it until it's absolutely necessary to give the baby the very best chance. In the meantime, we'll put her on steroids to help the foetus's lungs to mature.'

'I'll organise it,' she said. Remembering her

neighbour, she said quietly, 'Have you admitted a new patient this morning—Lily Harcourt? She's my neighbour. She would have come in by ambulance, suffering from pre-eclampsia? I wondered how she was doing. With any luck I'll be able to look in on her some time today, but I'm a bit concerned about her. She didn't look too good this morning.'

'She's your friend?' Lewis's dark eyes clouded. 'I'm sorry, I didn't know. Yes, she came to my ward. We have her on oxygen, and we're monitoring her heart and blood pressure. Unfortunately, she had a seizure when she first arrived, but we're giving her medication to control her blood pressure and also to try to prevent any more convulsions. It's too early for her to deliver this baby at the moment, so we need to get her condition stabilised.'

Ellie frowned, disturbed by his account. 'It doesn't sound good, does it?'

He laid an arm lightly about her shoulders. 'You shouldn't worry, Ellie. We're doing everything we can for her.'

'I know, I'm sure you are. Thanks, Lewis. Will you keep me updated?'

'Of course.' He gave her a quick hug and then headed back to the maternity ward. Ellie watched him go and then glanced across the room and saw James standing by the doorway, his eyes narrowed as he watched her.

How long had he been standing there? He must have seen Lewis put his arm around her, and for some reason he didn't look at all pleased. Was he bothered in some way about her friendship with his cousin?

She turned away. Why should she be concerned about what he was thinking? He may not have the same temperament as his father, but he obviously had the Birchenalls' way of taking control and keeping a check on everyone. He'd only been in the job five minutes and he was making sure he knew everything there was to know about the staff. She'd seen him looking at others in that calm, assessing way that seemed natural to him.

She looked in on Lily before she finished her

shift, and reassured her that she would take care of her little boy. Her friend still looked slightly flushed and seemed a bit restless, but that was probably because she was worried about her son.

'We'll come and see you as soon as the doctor says it's okay,' Ellie promised. 'In fact, I could get him to talk to you on the phone if that will make you feel better?'

'Oh, it would. Thanks, Ellie.'

'You're welcome.'

Ellie drove home, soothed by the beautiful Cheshire countryside, with its wooded hillsides and rolling plains. It helped put her in a relaxed frame of mind, so that for a little while she could forget that James Birchenall was a thorn in her side.

She stopped to pick up Jayden from his friend's house, and from then on any illusion of peace was shattered.

'Can we make play dough?' the four-year-old asked. 'I liked it when we did that before when I comed to your house.' He looked at her with shining grey eyes, full of eagerness and expectation.

'Okay. That sounds like a good idea.' Ellie remembered the last time, when loose bits of brightly coloured dough had escaped and gone off in all directions. She'd kept on finding bits of it all over the place for a couple of hours afterwards, mainly thanks to it being trampled underfoot by eager young feet. He'd even managed to get it tangled up among the curls in his dark hair.

'I thought we'd have spaghetti for tea. That's your favourite, isn't it?'

'Mmm. Yes. I always have s'ghetti. Every day.' He gave her a big-eyed look and she hid a smile.

'Do you? Really?'

'Yes.' He looked away uncertainly, as though he thought she might stop believing him if he held her gaze for too long.

'Well, we'll see what we can do. Let's go and collect your things from your house first and get you settled in.'

'All right.'

Some time later Ellie helped him to get ready for bed. They'd had a busy time, having fun with play dough, followed by a baking session, and by now she was worn out even if he wasn't.

'Mummy always tucks me in,' he said with a quiver in his voice, as he climbed into bed and looked around the strange room.

'I know, sweetheart, and I know she wishes she could be here with you now, but you talked to her on the phone, didn't you? Remember, she said she'll see you when we go to the hospital?'

He nodded solemnly, his eyes overbright.

'How about I read you a bedtime story?' Ellie said. 'Give teddy a cuddle and slide down under the duvet, and we'll see what Noddy's getting up to in his little red car.'

'Yeah.'

He'd fallen asleep before she finished the story, and Ellie switched off the bedside lamp and crept out of the room.

Downstairs, she cleared away Jayden's toys and tidied the kitchen, and just as she was thinking about making herself a well-earned cup of coffee, the doorbell rang. She frowned. She wasn't expecting anyone. Could it be Noah, in more trouble? Feeling apprehensive, she went to the door and found James standing there.

'Oh…I…um…'

He'd changed out of his suit, into casual, stylish clothes, stone-coloured chinos and a navy long-sleeved shirt, but there was still that air of authority about him. Somehow she sensed he wasn't there for a social visit. 'Is something wrong?'

'In a manner of speaking. Would it be all right if I come in? I don't mean to disturb you, but I need to talk to you about something and I'd prefer not to do it at the hospital.'

'Yes, of course.' He seemed serious, and she was troubled now, wondering what was so important that he'd come to see her at home. 'We'll go through to the kitchen and I'll put the coffee on.'

She led the way and waved him to a chair by the oak and granite topped table. 'It sounds as though I should be worried,' she said as she prepared the coffee. 'What's happened?' She put some freshly made fruit scones on a plate and passed it to him. 'Help yourself. There's butter and some strawberry jam.'

He looked at the golden-topped scones and smiled. 'A sample of your home baking? I thought there was a wonderful smell in the kitchen.' He sent her a quick, appreciative glance. 'How could I resist? Thanks. I haven't eaten yet this evening, so these will fill a hole.'

She raised her brows. 'You've not eaten? How did that come about?'

He shrugged. 'I was busy. I had a difficult case to deal with—a perforated appendix—and there were a couple of meetings I had to attend—one of them straight after my shift finished. It happens like that sometimes.' He cut a scone in half, spreading butter on each portion, and then added a spoonful of jam.

'Hmm. Perhaps you could introduce a snacks trolley so staff can grab a bite to eat if they can't make time to go to the restaurant. It shouldn't cost much and we could all chip in to fund it.'

She poured coffee and slid a cup towards him. She wasn't going to sit down. That would be too much like supping with the enemy.

'That's a good idea…a very good idea.' He bit into the scone and for a moment, as he chewed, a look of absorbed bliss came over his face. Ellie's breath caught in her throat. There was a boyish look about him that tugged at her heart and for a moment or two she floundered. 'These are delicious,' he said, smiling his satisfaction.

'Hmm.' She pulled herself together and studied him. 'Does that mean I get to keep my job?'

His brows met in puzzlement and she added, 'There was something you needed to tell me?'

'Ah.' He finished off the scone and swallowed some of the coffee. 'I wish I didn't have to tell you this, but…' He paused. 'Amelia Holt came into the hospital today and made a formal complaint. She believes her aunt didn't receive the proper care and attention she needed, resulting in her death.'

'Oh, no.' Ellie went pale, and felt for a seat opposite him, sitting down as her legs seemed to give way. 'I know she was upset, but what does she think I should have done?'

'She says you should have done a pericardiectomy. She's obviously been looking things up or talking to someone who knows a bit about medicine.'

'But that kind of surgery is usually a last resort.' Her mouth was dry and her heart had suddenly begun to thump heavily against her rib cage. She swallowed hard. 'Removing the pericardium is a risky procedure, and her aunt's heart was already weak.'

'I agree. It wouldn't have been the first course of action I'd have taken, but we have to acknowledge the complaint, I'm afraid.'

'So what happens now?' Ellie's palms were clammy, and she rubbed them against her jeans. Inside she was shaking.

'We have to set up a meeting with her to discuss the issue. If she accepts your viewpoint, there won't be anything more to be said, but if not, we have to take it through an independent review procedure.'

'All right. I understand. I…I just have to wait and see how…how things…'

He reached for her hand and captured it between his. 'Ellie, it's going to be all right. You've done nothing wrong.'

'I know, but…' The warmth of his caress comforted her, and for a while she lost herself in that gentle, yet firm, grasp. 'I still…'

'I'll go with you to the meeting, if that will help. You don't need to worry about this. I'm on your side.'

She nodded. 'Yes. I'd appreciate that. Thank you.'

He held her hand for a while longer, until she seemed to have calmed down. She let out a soft, shuddery sigh.

'Okay, then,' he said, gently releasing her. 'I'll arrange everything. Don't think about it again until the meeting.' His gaze meshed with hers. 'Promise me you'll cast it from your mind?'

'I'll try.' In spite of herself, she was already missing that warm embrace. Of course, she should never have let him comfort her—she didn't want to get close to the man whose father had destroyed her family. And yet...

'Good. I'm sorry I had to bring bad news.'

She nodded. 'I suppose we all have troubles to bear.' She glanced at him. 'I hear that things aren't so good for you back home. I know you said your father was unwell, but it's quite serious, isn't it?'

'His heart is failing, so life is difficult for him.' He braced his shoulders. 'It's not as bad as it sounds—as you know, people can live for years with heart failure. It's more a matter of quality of life that needs to be addressed.'

'Yes.' When someone's heart began to fail, it meant that the heart couldn't cope with pumping blood around the body, resulting in breathlessness, discomfort and fatigue.

'Still,' she said, 'he must be glad to have you back home. Are you living at the manor house?'

'I am.'

'And is that working out all right? You get on well with him, don't you?'

'Yes, I do.' He gave a wry smile. 'I'm his only

son and he's relying on me to take care of things and secure the family's heritage.'

She thought about that. 'I suppose you've had your career to keep you busy up till now. Becoming a consultant is a huge step.'

'It is.' He might have said something more, except that a small sound alerted them to the fact that they were no longer alone in the kitchen. They turned round.

Jayden stood in the doorway, clutching his teddy bear in the crook of his arm and rubbing his eye sleepily with his free hand. 'You putted the light out,' he said accusingly, looking at Ellie. 'I has to have the light on.'

Ellie hurried over to him and crouched down, bringing herself to his level. 'Oh, Jayden, sweetheart, I'm sorry.'

She'd turned the lamp out in case the light disturbed him. 'Let me take you back to bed. I'll leave your bedroom door open a little and put the hall light on. Will that be all right?'

The little boy nodded, and Ellie took hold of

his hand to gently lead him back upstairs. She glanced back at James. 'I won't be long.'

'That's okay.' He said it slowly and she saw that he was staring at Jayden in some kind of shock, his eyes wide, and a small frown creased his brow. Then he seemed to get himself together. 'Actually, uh…no need to rush. I should go. I have to go on to a dinner party.'

'Oh, I see. Of course…if you must.'

Jayden looked up at him. 'Who that?' he asked, holding onto Ellie's leg for protection as she stood up.

'I work with him at the hospital,' she told him quietly.

James made an effort to relax and said with a smile, 'Hello, Jayden.'

Jayden didn't answer, but gave him a cautious look from under his lashes.

'Come on,' Ellie murmured. 'Let's take you back to bed. You have to get up for school in the morning.' She glanced at James once more. 'Give me a minute and I'll see you out.'

'That's all right. I can see myself out. You go

ahead.' He walked towards the door. 'I'll see you tomorrow.'

'All right, then. Bye.' She couldn't quite understand the expression on his face, a mixture of disbelief and conjecture, and it was only after James had gone that it finally dawned on her... he thought Jayden was her child. But he'd gone, without giving her a chance to explain.

CHAPTER THREE

'IS THERE SOMETHING on your mind?' Lewis studied Ellie thoughtfully as they walked together towards A and E. 'What's wrong? Is it something to do with your TV programme? You look worried.'

'Do I?' Ellie covered her feelings with an attempt at a smile. 'No, I'm not worried. Everything's fine.' And that was true, at least as far as her TV career was concerned. She was to record the next programme in the series in a few days' time.

As to the rest, things were unravelling fast, and she couldn't begin to tell him about that—where would she start? With the fact that in the last few days she'd discovered that her hospital career was under a cloud, or that her boss was the very last person she'd want to work with?

Or maybe she could blame her troubles on the cryptic text message she'd received from Noah that morning—one that had left her wondering what on earth was about to explode in her face and cause all manner of fallout. He must have sent it yesterday, but she'd been busy looking after Jayden and hadn't checked her messages.

Things are on the up and up. Just had a huge scoop—the Sunday Supplement printed my article and photo exposé about the Birchenalls. Will get a copy to you.

Despite her bad feelings towards Lord Birchenall, she would never have condoned putting forward any piece of writing that drew a negative picture of his family. It wasn't in her to take that kind of revenge.

Unfortunately, though, it looked as though she was too late to put the brakes on Noah. Today was Monday, which meant the paper had already gone out. Whatever the article contained, it didn't sound good, and she could only hope James hadn't seen it.

'Is it to do with your meeting with Amelia Holt tomorrow?' Lewis persisted. 'It must be on your mind.'

'I suppose it is, but I'm trying not to think about it.'

'I can understand that.' He glanced at her. 'Perhaps we could have lunch together tomorrow, and you can tell me all about it?

She nodded. She certainly didn't want to talk about any of her problems to Lewis, though, so she did her best to change the subject as they walked into the emergency unit.

'How is Lily getting on?' she asked. 'I went to see her over the weekend, and although she hid it from Jayden, it seemed to me she was a bit down.'

Jayden had been overjoyed to see his mother. He'd given her a picture he'd made, showing her sitting up in bed, with a teddy bear of her own to cheer her up. He'd beamed brightly when she'd given him a hug and a kiss in exchange.

Lewis pulled a face. 'It's only to be expected, I suppose. She has an intravenous drip to contend with, she's not enjoying the enforced rest, and she wants to be with her child. And, of course, her husband's still away. That can't be good for her peace of mind, and it has a bad effect on her blood pressure.'

Ellie frowned. 'He offered to come straight home from Switzerland to be with her, but she was worried about the effect on the business. He owns the company, so it's their livelihood. Unfortunately he's had to deal with a lot of difficult situations in the Swiss branch lately.'

'That's bound to cause a conflict of loyalties, I suppose.'

She nodded. 'I told her I'm okay looking after Jayden, and she hasn't gone into labour, so she told him to finish what he went there for. He says he's going to come over here to be with her and then go back to work next day. Of course, they talk all the time on the phone, so that helps.'

'Well, we seem to have stabilised her condition for now, but I'm keeping her on bed rest—her blood pressure does vary and we need to keep it down. As soon as I feel the time is right, we'll deliver her baby by Caesarean section.'

'At least I know she's in safe hands.'

He smiled and said teasingly, 'You know I'm taking extra-special care of her just because she's your friend.'

Ellie laughed and they parted company as she set out to work her way down her list of patients and Lewis went off to answer his pager call.

James watched her approach the desk. He was there looking through a sheaf of papers, and as she came closer she saw they were lab reports.

'Hi, there,' she greeted him, but he only nodded in return, his eyes half-closed as he watched Lewis head towards one of the treatment bays. She looked at him in confusion. That wasn't the reaction she'd expected. Again she had the feeling that there was some reason he didn't want her being friendly with Lewis. Or was there something more to it?

'I have to go out,' he said, 'so perhaps you could deal with the angina patient in room three?' His tone was curt and she sent him a quick glance. His whole body was taut, she noticed, and a muscle was flexing in his jaw.

'Okay.' She frowned. 'Will you be coming back at all today?'

'I don't know. My father was taken ill yesterday, and just now I had a call to say he's taken a turn for the worse. I have to go and be with him.'

'Oh, I'm so sorry,' she said, a flood of sympathy washing over her. 'That must be worrying for you.' A horrible thought struck her. Had he seen the Sunday papers?

He didn't answer her, but his smoke-dark gaze met hers like the lash of a whip, and she felt her throat go dry.

'James…'

'I've examined the patient briefly and he has unstable angina. He'll probably need to be scheduled for cardiac catheterisation as soon as possible. I've given him blood-thinning medication, but he'll need a beta-blocker and—'

'I'll see to it,' she cut in. 'Really, you don't need to be concerned. I'll do everything necessary.' Didn't he trust her? Was he having second thoughts about her competency now that Mel had made an official complaint?

'I'm not concerned. Not about that, at any rate.'

'Then what is it that's troubling you?'

'Perhaps you should talk to your brother about that. His article in the Sunday paper wasn't even based on truth—my father's business dealings are all above board. He would never harass anyone. And as for myself, what gives him the right to lay out my private life in the tabloids for all to see? What he did was irresponsible—unforgivable—especially given my father's precarious state of health.'

He dropped the papers back in the tray and strode away before she could answer him. All at once her stomach felt like lead. So he *had* seen the newspaper. Now, more than ever, she wanted to know what Noah had written.

'He's well and truly put out, isn't he?' Olivia said, frowning, as she came to look at a patient's file. She pushed a stray lock of fair hair behind her ear. 'I've not seen him like that before—

mind you, if you've seen the paper… I guess you must have—there's a copy in the staff lounge.'

'I haven't seen it,' Ellie answered quietly. 'What's it all about?'

'Well, it's to do with both him and his father. James has this upper-crust girlfriend, Sophie Granger—'

'He does?' Unexpectedly, Ellie's heart plummeted. It hadn't occurred to her that James was spoken for. But why would he not be involved? After all, he was an extremely eligible man.

Olivia nodded. 'She's from a well-to-do family—you know the sort of thing, born to money. They're close friends of the Birchenalls, apparently. Anyway, there were several photos of him with her, but then there are also pictures of him leaving a private dinner party with another beautiful young woman. The article sort of makes him sound like a philanderer.'

Ellie absorbed all that. Perhaps there was no truth in any of it. Her brother might have seen James with these women and made up his own mind about what was going on. On the other hand, she'd already had one bad experience with her ex. Shouldn't she have learned a lesson from that? How was James any different from him?

'And his father? What does the article say about him?'

Olivia winced. 'It makes him out to be a ruthless businessman. Apparently he's been trying to obtain some land from his neighbour so that he can expand the dairy farm and add more trees to the orchard. The only problem is, the owner of the land doesn't want to part with it, and complains he's being harassed.'

'Oh, dear.' Ellie groaned inwardly. What had Noah been thinking? He must have followed James over the last few days in order to get this scoop, and had somehow managed to delve into his father's business dealings.

'I feel sorry for James,' Olivia said. 'He's not been here long, but he's been fair to everyone and treated us well. He's always there to listen if you need to talk.' She smiled. 'He's even started to bring in cakes and pasties for when we need to grab a quick bite to eat. I asked him who's paying for it, and he said he was.'

Ellie closed her eyes briefly. Was she wrong to see James as the enemy? His father had hurt her family badly, but was that anything to do with James? She would have to try to do something to put this right. Maybe if her neighbour could keep Jayden for a little longer this evening, she should pay James a visit. She would give her a call and find out.

She'd no idea what she would say to James, but surely she had no choice but to try to make amends? She had to work with him, after all.

And as to Noah… He'd never behaved this way before. Did his dislike of the Birchenalls go so deep that he would go against his principles? Maybe in the cool light of day he would come to regret what he had done.

As soon as she found time to take a break, she called him. 'What were you thinking, Noah, going ahead with a piece like that? Don't you realise how much trouble you've caused?'

'I just took advantage of circumstances,' Noah

protested. 'I was in the area and I saw Birchenall standing there with his arm around this pretty young woman. It's exactly the sort of thing that sells.' She could feel the frown in his voice. 'I thought you'd be pleased. It means I can pay you back the money you loaned me.'

'How could I be pleased? You said yourself Lord Birchenall has a bad heart. How did you think he would be affected by what you wrote? And as for myself—James is my boss! I have to work with him. Heaven knows how far this has set us back.'

'He'll come round.' Noah shrugged it off. 'His kind of people are used to this sort of thing. They're in the public eye all the time.'

It was clear he didn't understand her point of view, and eventually Ellie cut the call, feeling more disturbed than ever. She would have to do something to try and smooth things over.

When her shift finished at the end of the afternoon, she checked on Jayden at her friend's house, and then hurried home to change into something presentable. It was important that she look her best, because she had to muster all the confidence she possessed if she was to face up to both James and his father.

In the end, she chose a midnight-blue dress that swathed her figure in gentle folds, and added a light touch of make-up to lend a soft flush of colour to her cheeks. Her hair fell loosely about her shoulders, the silky, chestnut curls gleaming with health.

It was several years since she'd been anywhere near her former home, and as she drove along the Birchenalls' sweeping drive in the early evening, memories of her childhood came flooding back.

Her family had lived in the lodge, a neat cottage situated in the grounds, and she'd spent the summers exploring the surrounding woods with her friends. They'd fished for tiddlers in the brook that ran through the estate, and picked wild flowers in the meadows. They had been blissful times, until her father had lost his way and their world had fallen apart.

The manor house came into view and she gazed at it with a mixture of awe and apprehension. How would James and her father respond to her turning up here? She would be their least favourite person at the moment.

She drew the car to a halt on the cobbled drive and stepped out to look around. She'd always loved this beautiful old house, with its white-painted walls and pretty leaded windows. The building was wide and symmetrical, with an extended middle portion whose tiled roof met at right angles with the main roof structure. In front of that was a large covered porch, again with its own roof canopy.

Steeling herself, she approached the front door and rang the bell. Then she waited, her heart beginning to pound. Why on earth was she feeling so nervous? There was no explanation, except that perhaps this place—and its owner—had been at the root of all her family's troubles.

'Ellie?' James frowned when he opened the door then pulled it wider. He was wearing dark chinos and a shirt that was open at the neck to reveal his lightly bronzed throat.

Ellie swallowed and tried to work out what she was going to say.

His gaze ran over her briefly as he tried to read her expression. 'Has something happened at the hospital—something I need to know about?'

'No, not at all,' she said quickly. 'It's nothing like that.' She hesitated. 'I just wanted to know if your father had recovered at all? I felt I had to come here and say how sorry I am that my brother caused you and your father any distress. I don't think—'

'Come in,' he said. He ushered her into a large hallway and then led the way to a sitting room. In here, the evening sunlight filtered through diamond panes of glass, glinting on crystal vases and fluted goblets set out in a display cabinet. Table lamps shed small pools of golden light over mahogany occasional tables, and lit up the open fireplace where an original oak beam formed the main feature. Overhead there were more beams, lending an old-world look to the room.

'How is your father?' she asked.

'He had a nasty setback, but thankfully he's feeling much better now.'

'Can I ask what happened?'

He nodded. 'I think the stress of reading the article overloaded his heart, so that he had trouble getting his breath. I gave him oxygen and medication to relieve the symptoms. It took a while, but eventually he began to pull round. Then today he was bombarded with calls from the press. They even camped out on the driveway.'

She frowned. 'I didn't see anyone out there.'

'No. I called the police and had them moved on.' His expression was bleak. 'My father can't take the strain these days.'

'No. I realise that. I feel bad about all this. I don't think Noah really understood the implications of what he was doing.'

'Hmm.' His glance shimmered over her, taking in her worried look and the silent plea in her green eyes. He laid a finger gently under her chin. 'It's actually Noah who should be here apologising. You didn't need to take it on yourself to come here in his place.'

'N-no...' She stumbled over her words, distracted by the soothing touch of his hand. It was almost like a caress. 'But I felt it was necessary. I would never have wanted this to happen.'

He released her and went over to a cabinet at the side of the room. 'Can I get you a drink?'

She shook her head. 'I'm driving but thanks. Maybe a juice of some sort if you have it.' Her mouth was dry and she needed some kind of pick-me-up.

'Okay.' He took out a tall glass and added a generous portion of ice, topping it up with fruit juice. He handed it to her with a paper coaster and poured himself a small measure of whisky.

She looked around the room. 'This is a lovely room. It seems strange, but I don't think I've ever been in this house more than a few times over the years,' she murmured. 'I would go to the back entrance when I had messages to pass on from my father, and your housekeeper would slip me a cookie or a fruit tart if she'd been baking. I think it's down to her that I developed the urge to learn to cook.'

He smiled. 'Harriet's still with us, though she works fewer hours now. I'm very fond of her. She took me under her wing and helped me a lot after my mother died. She became like a second mother to me.'

Ellie nodded. 'I remember how kind she was.' She hesitated. 'I noticed there are some pictures of your mother around the room. You couldn't have been very old when she died.'

'No. I was ten or eleven.'

Ellie's heart went out to that young boy who must have been through so much anguish. 'That must have come as a real shock to you.'

'Yes, it did, though she'd been ill for some time, and I remember wishing that I knew more about medicine so that I could make her better.'

Ellie laid her hand gently on his arm. 'I can't imagine how awful that must have been for you.'

His expression was wistful, acknowledging her compassion. 'Perhaps there was a silver lining, after all. I guess that's what made me decide to become a doctor.'

She nodded and let her hand slide away from him. 'How did your father react to that decision? I imagine he would have preferred you to stay here and run the estate when you were of age.'

'That's right, he did. It caused a few problems to begin with. But, going back, I think my mother's passing had a huge effect on my father. He became bitter and more intolerant of other people.'

'I think I can see how that would happen.' So perhaps that was why he'd let her father go without a second thought?

The door opened then and to her dismay Lord Birchenall came into the room. He had steel-grey hair and regular features, and Ellie noticed that he walked with a slight stoop.

'James,' he said, then stopped suddenly as he saw Ellie standing there. 'Ah, I thought I heard voices.' He looked her over, his dark eyes assessing, missing nothing. 'I don't think I have had the pleasure,' he said with a smile. He glanced towards his son, clearly expecting an introduction.

James inclined his head a fraction. 'This is Ellie,' he responded. 'She's changed quite a lot over the years, so you perhaps won't remember her but she's John Saunders's daughter.'

Lord Birchenall stiffened. His jaw clenched and he turned his attention back to Ellie, saying tersely, 'I can't imagine why you would show your face here after the piece your brother wrote about us.' His breath rasped in his lungs, and the colour rose alarmingly in his cheeks.

She was taken aback by the vehemence of his words but she tried to ignore his obvious hostility. 'I haven't read the article,' she said, 'but I do understand that it must have been upsetting for you.'

He gave a snort of derision.

Ellie pulled in a deep breath and started again. 'I came here to apologise for my brother's actions. I don't think he thought things through. You must understand that he feels a lot of resentment towards you after what happened to our father. I think he seized an opportunity to tip the scales, as it were.'

Lord Birchenall's brows rose sharply in angry disbelief and she hurried to add, 'I'm not condoning what he did in any way, but I'm just trying to explain what might lie behind it.'

'Why would he choose to do this now, after all this time?'

Ellie moved restlessly, suddenly uncomfortable. 'I think it was because James...because your son started to work at the hospital with me. It has thrown us into close contact after all this time, and it seems to have stirred everything up again.'

She hesitated then went on. 'Noah was quite young when my father lost his job and it had a huge effect on him. Perhaps now, as an adult, he felt the need to express his feelings. But I realise that you've been ill and I'm sorry that he hurt you.'

'Hmmph.' Clearly Lord Birchenall wasn't appeased. His eyes narrowed on her. 'I remember you now. You're that wayward little madam who ran amok through the village, getting into all sorts of trouble after you left here. I suppose you'll say that was my fault, too?'

Ellie's face paled. It was true her behaviour had deteriorated badly when their family life had fallen apart. But she hadn't been expecting that full-on assault and she didn't know how to answer him.

James stepped forward. 'Ellie came here to apologise,' he said in a quiet reprimand. 'I don't see that there's any need to add more fuel to the fire.'

Lord Birchenall ignored him and pressed on. 'Your father simply didn't do his job properly,' he told her. 'He was warned what would happen if his work didn't improve, but he chose to ignore those warnings.' He struggled to get his breath. 'Whatever happened is on his head.'

Ellie braced her shoulders. She was very conscious that this man was unwell, and she didn't want to exacerbate that situation in any way, but she was goaded into defending her father.

'He worked for you for many years without a

problem. If his behaviour became erratic after that, there had to be a reason and the truth is he was ill. That's what caused things to go wrong, and being dismissed and thrown out of his house with no means of fending for his family led him on a downward spiral.'

His mouth flattened. 'I'd have expected you to make excuses for him.'

He turned away from her, glancing at his son. 'I came in here to tell you that Sophie phoned earlier when you were out.' Becoming unsteady on his feet, he began to reach behind him for a chair, and James came forward to lend him a supporting arm.

He sat down, taking a moment to pull air into his lungs. 'She's upset about the article, too, so I persuaded her to come along and have dinner with us. We'll have to do our best to sort things out.'

James frowned. 'I'm sure Sophie won't be upset for long.'

Ellie's stomach clenched involuntarily. He didn't seem too concerned. Maybe he was con-

fident enough in his relationship with his girlfriend to be certain he could smooth things over
with her. That thought made her feel strangely
out of sorts.

'I think I'd better go,' she said, putting down
her empty glass. 'I have to pick up Jayden from
a friend's house.'

'Of course.' He glanced at her left hand and
must have seen that it was bare of rings. He
seemed puzzled, but she was in no mood to explain things, especially with his father looking
on.

She wasn't sure quite what she'd achieved
by coming here. Lord Birchenall was still ag-
grieved, and it looked as though she was in the
way because James was about to get ready to
greet his girlfriend.

'Goodbye, Lord Birchenall.'

He nodded. 'Goodbye, Miss Saunders.'

'It's actually Dr Saunders,' James murmured,
but his father didn't bother to acknowledge that
comment.

James took Ellie lightly by the elbow and led

her to the hallway. 'I'm sorry about the way my father spoke to you,' he said as they walked to the door.

'It's all right.' His hand on her arm was comforting, and for one wild moment she wished she could turn to him and let him soothe away all her problems. Of course, it would never happen.

James gazed down at her. 'He's always been very forthright—I'm afraid it's a quality that can be both a blessing and a curse.'

'Yes, I imagine it is.' She half turned towards the door. 'Goodbye, James.'

'Goodbye.' He held open the door for her and she stepped out onto the porch. She was desperate to leave.

More and more she was seeing that it had been a mistake to come here. Perhaps in a naive way she had been hoping for some kind of redemption, but instead she felt more dejected than ever.

It was odd, because she had no idea why she was feeling that way.

CHAPTER FOUR

'WHEN'S MY MUMMY coming home?' Jayden spooned breakfast cereal into his mouth and looked at Ellie with wide grey eyes.

Ellie made a small start. Her thoughts had been far away, with James and the way her body responded to his slightest touch. It was disturbing to have so little control over her emotions and she would have to guard against that. After all, he had a girlfriend. It ought not to have bothered her to discover that, but it had.

She met Jayden's innocent gaze and decided it was best to be truthful. 'I'm not sure,' she told him. 'But she's feeling a lot better now, and once the new baby is born it won't be long before they'll both be able to come home.'

He pulled a face. 'Why can't she leave it at the hospital?'

Ellie's brows shot up. 'Do you want her to do that?'

He nodded.

'But why?'

'I don't want Mummy to have a baby,' he said, wriggling his shoulders. 'Why can't she just give it to a nurse?'

'Um, I really don't think she would want to do that.' She looked at him in consternation. 'Are you sure you don't want a little brother or a sister? After all, it might be quite nice for you when it's a bit older. You'll have someone special to play with.'

He wrinkled his nose. 'I don't want anyone else to play with. I like playing with Josh.'

'Well, I'm glad you get on well with him,' she said. Jayden went to school with Josh, her neighbour's child, every day, so it was good that they'd forged such a strong friendship.

She stood up and affectionately stroked his hair. This was a difficult one, and maybe it was something she had better not share with his mother just yet. The way things were going, she might have a few days yet to bring him round to accepting the status quo.

A short time later she dropped him off at her neighbour's house and kissed him goodbye. Molly was good with children and she knew she could relax, leaving her to take him and Josh to nursery school.

Jayden's reluctance to accept the new baby was on her mind, though, as she drove to work, and when she arrived at A and E she told Olivia what he'd said.

'At least he's come out into the open with it,' Olivia commented. 'It could be worse, I suppose, if he were to bottle it all up. You hear such stories about children being jealous of their siblings.'

Ellie nodded in agreement. 'I wish I could find some way to help him get over it.'

At least her discussion with Jayden had helped take her mind off the meeting she had to attend later that morning. Amelia Holt was coming to the hospital so that they could discuss her complaint, and every time she thought about it, her insides lurched. No matter how convinced she was that she'd done everything possible to save Mel's aunt, if this complaint was taken further to a second hearing there was always the chance that her career could be badly damaged.

Through the course of the morning she became more and more apprehensive. James had said he would be with her when the time came, and that helped, but it also added to her confusion. Her emotions were all over the place where he was concerned.

She forced herself to concentrate on her work and later, as she was passing by one of the treatment rooms, she saw that James was working on his own in there.

He was talking to his patient, a man who had been vomiting and was now struggling to breathe. It was clear that James was doing his best to make him feel better. Beads of sweat had broken out on the man's brow. He looked very ill and as though he was in great pain, and Ellie could see from the monitors that his heartbeat was very fast and his blood pressure was dropping.

All the time James was gentle and supportive and Ellie stood still for a moment, struck by his caring manner.

Then, all at once, things started to change. The man appeared to collapse suddenly and monitors all around him started to make shrill bleeping sounds. Ellie hurried into the room.

'Would you like some help?' she asked.

'Thanks.' James was reaching for the intubation equipment.

'What are we dealing with here?'

'I suspect from his history that it's acute pancreatitis—he was complaining of abdominal pain and continual vomiting.' He frowned. 'He looks anorexic.'

'Yes, he does, except for the swelling of his abdomen.'

'Will you put in a nasogastric tube?' James asked as soon as the patient was intubated. 'He's been vomiting so much I need to be sure he's not going to choke.'

She nodded. 'I will.'

She set to work, and as soon as he was sure that the man was receiving adequate oxygen and was connected to the ventilator, James prepared his patient and began to insert two central lines so that he could be given medication and other essential substances.

'He's dehydrated,' he said. 'At this rate, his kidneys will start to fail—we need to get him on normal saline right away.'

She nodded. 'I'll set up a drip. Has he had a painkiller?' She checked the man's notes. His name was David Langley and within the last month he'd been to his GP complaining of abdominal pain.

'I'm doing that now. I'm going with meperidine.'

Watching him at work, Ellie could see why he'd reached the level of consultant. He was exceptionally skilful and thorough in everything he did. She sighed inwardly. If only she could share some of his calm expertise. Ever since Grace Holt had died, she had begun to question everything she did. Even something like placing a catheter could be hazardous if the correct sterile techniques weren't followed.

'Are you okay with helping me?' James was watching her, and she guessed he was wondering about her hesitation.

'Yes. I'm all right.'

She dragged her thoughts back to the task in hand and started to insert a catheter into the man's arm. As soon as that was done, she set up the saline bag, hooking it up to a metal stand. Then she connected the IV tubing to the catheter and checked that the infusion was working correctly.

Once they had seen to their patient's immediate needs, James said, 'I'll get a CT scan done. It's possible that gallstones have passed into the bile duct and caused the inflammation, but from his condition I suspect there's a lot more going on here.'

'Like what?'

'Maybe an abscess and certainly general inflammation. If that turns out to be the case, we'll have to drain it, but I'm going to give him a strong antibiotic as a precaution. I'm pretty sure there's an infection of some sort. Anyway, I'll take him along to Radiology.'

He glanced at her. 'You're very quiet. Are you sure you're all right?'

'I'm fine.'

'Good.' He scanned her features a moment longer as though he still had some doubts. 'As soon as I've finished here, I'll help you prepare for the meeting with Miss Holt. Whatever happens, remember that you did the right thing. It's not your fault that her aunt died.'

She nodded. For a few minutes as they'd worked she'd been able to forget about it, but now her anxiety had come back with full force.

He glanced at his watch. 'It's not for another hour yet. We should have plenty of time.'

He went off to Radiology with Mr Langley, while Ellie returned to her own patients.

When it was almost time for the meeting, she handed over to another registrar and went to seek out James once more. She was feeling jittery and wishing their appointment was over and done with.

'Do you have Mr Langley's results?' she asked.

James nodded. 'Yes, I have the radiology report and some of the lab tests are back. Alongside the bile duct obstruction there's a large abscess resulting from infection of fluid that has collected in the abdomen.'

He glanced at the patient's chart. 'I've put in a drain tube to draw off the infected matter and called for a surgical consultation. A renal specialist is going to come down and look at him, too.'

She frowned. 'He's not doing very well, is he?'

'No.' He shook his head. 'I've arranged for him to be transferred to Intensive Care as soon as we can manage it.' He glanced at her. 'You're very pale. Are you worried about seeing your schoolfriend?'

'I don't think she thinks of herself as a friend any longer.' She guessed he could read her body language and she made an effort to calm herself.

'I'm a bit apprehensive,' she admitted. 'I've been trying not to think about it all morning.'

He lightly squeezed her hand. 'I'll be there with you,' he said. 'Between us, we should be able to persuade the woman that there's no case to pursue.'

'I hope so.' She appreciated him trying to cheer her up. It made her feel a lot better, but she wasn't as confident as he was that Amelia would be easily appeased. She'd always been a volatile, over-emotional person and her love for her aunt had made her fiercely defensive.

'Try not to worry.'

'I'll try.' She glanced at him. His smile was encouraging, coaxing her to have faith, and it warmed her inside to know that he was such a caring, thoughtful man. How was it that he could be so different from his father?

She hesitated as he glanced through the radiology report. 'How is your father?' she asked after a while. 'I hope he hasn't had any more setbacks. I was a bit worried I might have done more harm than good when I went to the manor house yesterday.'

'Is that what's been bothering you?' He made a wry face. 'None of it was your fault, and I'm sorry he spoke to you the way he did. He's been more tetchy of late and I think that's down to his illness. His heart has been failing for some time, and he isn't used to being so restricted and helpless. I've come to realise that all I can do is try to make his life more tolerable. It grieves me that it's come to this, but in the end we just have to make the best of things.'

'I realise it must be difficult for him. I have to remind myself that he's ill and I need to make allowances.'

He laid the report down in the wire basket. 'Let's go to my office,' he suggested.

She went with him along the corridor to a room that looked out over a large quadrangle, decorated with tubs of colourful flowers, pretty fuchsias and scarlet geraniums.

His office was furnished with a large, polished mahogany table and three comfortable leather-backed chairs, and on the walls were a couple of watercolour paintings showing peaceful country landscapes. It was a restful room, and Ellie imagined that patients and their relatives would soon begin to feel at their ease in here.

James poured coffee from a machine at the side of the room and handed her a cup. 'Help yourself to cream and sugar,' he said. 'It might be a good idea to eat something, too.' He took a packet of biscuits down from a wall cupboard and tipped some of them out onto a plate. 'Food might calm your nerves.'

'Thank you.' She didn't feel like eating, but it was thoughtful of him to offer.

'How are your parents these days?' he asked, coming to sit down opposite her, and she had the feeling he was trying to divert her thoughts from the meeting ahead.

'My father is working as an estate manager again,' she told him. 'It's nowhere near as large as the Birchenall estate, but he seems happy there.' She paused, swallowing her coffee. 'I see him often—he comes over to the house for dinner with me and Noah and vice versa.'

'And your mother?' he prompted.

'I haven't seen her for some time,' she murmured. 'She went into a deep depression when we had to leave the lodge, but after a while she was admitted to hospital and had some treatment that seemed to help. Then, when she was back on her feet, she moved away from Cheshire to a small village in Wales. We didn't have much contact with her after that. I don't think she could handle the responsibility of a family.'

'I'm sorry.' He was quiet for a moment, deep in thought. 'Perhaps that's why you went off the rails for a while? It must have been really hard to bear when your mother left.'

Her cheeks flushed with heat. 'It was, though she gave Noah and me a choice. We could have gone with her, but she had never seemed to have our interests at heart. Whereas my father has always been a loving man, despite his problems, so we both decided to stay with him. It's something I don't like to think about too much. And I did behave badly afterwards, I admit. I rebelled against everything. Your father was quite right when he pointed it out.'

Perhaps the biggest legacy of that time was her feeling that no one was to be trusted with her heart. It had been shattered by her mother, the one person who should have cared most of all, so how could she rely on anyone else to cherish her?

And back then, filled with feelings of rejection and despair, she'd responded by running amok and getting into as much trouble as she possibly could.

James gave a faint shrug. 'My father didn't look for reasons back then, and I don't recall too many of the details. Like I said, I went away round about that time. Wasn't it something to do with drink and wild stunts? Late-night partying and that sort of thing?'

'Something like that,' she murmured. She shuddered, thinking of a couple of times when her exploits had been featured in the local paper.

He frowned. 'It must have been difficult for

you. I know something of what it's like to lose a mother, but I had my father and Harriet to help me through the bad times. Does your mother still not keep in touch?'

'No, not really. An occasional note and maybe a card at Christmas.'

Just then there was a knock at the door and a nurse showed Amelia Holt into the room.

She seemed tense, obviously uptight, and though Ellie stood up and went to greet her, Amelia didn't make eye contact. Her black hair was cut in a tidy, layered bob, and she wore a dark blue suit with a jacket nipped in at the waist. She looked neat and businesslike.

James did his best to put her at ease. 'We're here to try to understand the nature of your complaint and see what we can do to sort things out,' he said, after inviting her to sit down and offering her a cup of coffee. 'I'm hoping that we might be able to resolve the situation to everyone's satisfaction.'

They talked at length, but it soon became clear that Amelia was adamant in going ahead with her complaint. 'I know that if more had been done for my aunt, she would be alive now. I accept that she was very ill but if Dr Saunders had acted sooner, things would have turned out very differently.'

James frowned. 'I've read through the medical notes that were made that day,' he said, taking out Grace Holt's file and skimming through its contents, 'and I have to say I feel that Dr Saunders acted in the best interests of your aunt. She worked very quickly to diagnose the nature of the problem and then followed all the treatment protocols. I'm very sorry—we're both sorry—that your aunt is no longer with us, but I don't believe Dr Saunders could have done anything more to save her.'

'I'm not satisfied,' Amelia said, pressing her lips together. 'I want to take this further. I want the matter to be dealt with by somebody who is completely independent.'

'That is your prerogative, of course.'

Ellie felt a wave of nausea rise in her stomach. This business could go on for months, and all that time she would be under a cloud. Would her colleagues begin to talk among themselves and start to ask what it was that she'd done wrong?

'It's what I want,' Amelia insisted. She stood up, preparing to leave. 'You'll let me know when the next hearing is to take place?'

James and Ellie stood up. 'I will,' James said. He showed Amelia to the door and she left without looking back.

Ellie curled her fingers into a tight ball in her lap. Her one-time friend hadn't once looked at her.

James shut the door and came back to her. 'Well, that could have gone better,' he said in a rueful voice.

Ellie nodded, but couldn't bring herself to say anything just then. She bent her head as though that would shut out all that had just happened, and her chestnut curls momentarily fell across her cheeks and hid her face. She was glad James could not see her desperation. In the back of her mind she'd hoped that by talking things through with them Mel would come to see sense, but without a doubt that wasn't going to happen, now or in the future.

'I can see you're upset,' James said. He laid an arm around her shoulders, and she lifted her head, raising a shaky hand to brush the hair back from her cheeks. 'I'm sure it's not nearly as bad as it seems,' he went on. 'No one in the medical profession is going to decide in her favour. You did everything you could to save Mrs Holt.' He gave her an encouraging smile. 'Why don't we go and have lunch and see if we can't talk this through?'

'Mel seemed so determined,' she said quietly. 'It seems hard to believe that we were once friends, that we went to school together. We used to confide in one another and she'd comfort me whenever I was in trouble.'

'It's the shock of losing a loved one.' He reached for her hand. 'Lunch?' he said again.

'I'd like that but I can't,' she said, suddenly remembering that she'd arranged to meet Lewis. She was disappointed. She wanted to go with James, so that they could spend some more time together. He seemed to understand her and was there for her, and that made her feel good inside.

'I'm supposed to be meeting Lewis,' she said, conscious of his hand engulfing hers. 'He said he wants to hear how the meeting went, and I'm hoping he'll be able to give me news about one of his patients...my neighbour. I've been really worried about her. She was admitted with pre-eclampsia and I think he might be doing a Caesarean soon.'

James frowned. 'Are you sure it's wise for him to do that?'

'A Caesarean?'

'To discuss a patient's details.'

'Oh, I see.' She shook her head. 'It'll be all right. He won't tell me any confidential details.'

He studied her, his expression brooding. 'You see a lot of Lewis, don't you? He seems to be a good friend.'

She nodded. 'He is. We've known each other for a long time.' She studied him closely. 'Is that a problem for you?'

'I'm not sure. Do you think he might be getting a little too fond of you?'

She stared at him. 'What do you mean?'

'Well, he seems to be very familiar with you.' His gaze meshed with hers. 'Perhaps you don't notice it.'

'No, I don't. I haven't.' Her brows met in a worried line.

'Hmm.' He sounded as though he didn't believe her. 'You know his marriage is in trouble, don't you?'

Her mouth dropped open a little. There had been rumours, but she'd taken no notice of them. If Lewis had any problems, she was sure he would manage to sort them out somehow. 'I imagine all couples have their ups and downs. You're adding two and two together and making five.'

'I don't think so. I'm simply telling you what I see, and I'm asking you to steer clear of getting too deeply involved with him. He's my cousin, and I care for him like a brother—I don't want to see him get hurt. He's vulnerable right now, and if you give him half a chance, he might do something he'll come to regret.'

She gave a small gasp, pulling her hand away from his as though she'd been scalded. 'You're warning me off? How can you say such things to me? Do you really think I would get involved with a married man?'

'I was just offering some friendly advice,' he said quietly. His eyes scanned her face. 'I'm concerned about him. The grapevine is already buzzing with rumours about you and him being together—I wouldn't want either of you to be hurt, that's all.'

There were rumours going around? She stiffened. 'Thank you for your concern, but I'm quite capable of conducting my own relationships without any help from you—and so is Lewis. Whatever we do, it's certainly no business of yours—cousin or no cousin.'

She wrenched open the door and went out into the corridor. How could he even suggest that she was involved with Lewis in that way?

She was still angry when she walked into the

cafeteria a few minutes later, but she made a supreme effort to calm down as she picked up a tray and loaded it with various items of food. She'd been a fool to allow herself to be pulled into James's web of charm. She might have known it would come back to hit her in the face.

'Hi, Ellie.' Lewis put his tray down on the table and came to sit opposite her. 'I've had a really difficult morning. My placenta praevia patient had another bleed and I had to take her to Theatre straight away. It was either that or risk losing the baby.'

'Phoebe? What happened?' She was shocked. 'Are they both all right?'

He nodded. 'Thankfully, yes. Phoebe needed a transfusion, but she seems to be rallying now. The baby's fine. A bit of a concern to us at first, but he's okay now.'

She smiled. 'That's good to hear.' She dipped a fork into her lasagne. 'Is there any news on Lily? I don't like to ask her too much when I visit, especially with Jayden listening in.'

He grimaced. 'I'd prefer it if I could say she

was completely free of symptoms, but she still needs to be closely monitored for the usual things: blood pressure and protein in the urine. It's still a tad too early for us to elect to deliver the baby, so we're being very careful with her.'

'She hasn't had any more seizures, though?'

'No. We have her on medication to try and prevent those.'

She talked to Lewis for a while longer, and all the time she was asking herself if what James had said could possibly be true. Was Lewis being over-familiar with her? She couldn't see any evidence of it, though, and made up her mind to dismiss it from her thoughts.

'I should go,' she said, glancing at her watch. 'I'm due back in A and E.'

Lewis smiled. 'It wouldn't do for you to be tardy and have your new boss put a black mark against your name, would it?'

She gave a wry smile. It was a bit too late for her to worry about that, wasn't it? James must have tacked her outburst onto the list of reasons why she was a difficult person to have on his team. He already had a number of items on that list! In the short time he'd been here he'd learned that a complaint had been made against her, she'd upset his father, and he'd discovered she was subject to quick bursts of temper.

She didn't see James for the rest of the afternoon. He and the senior house officer were dealing with a crush injury, leaving her to tend to a girl who had broken her ankle.

She left for home at the end of her shift feeling weary and out of sorts, and when Noah rang just as she arrived home he picked up on her mood. 'Are things not going well?' he asked.

'You could say that.' She told him what had happened.

'Do you think you might be reading too much into what he says? After all, you've a lot on your plate just now, what with looking after Jayden and the TV work, and so on—maybe you're a bit stressed?'

'Maybe.'

They talked for a while longer, and when she finally cut the call she was at least reassured that his career was on the up and up. 'I'm getting lots of commissions now,' he'd told her. 'The tide seems to have turned in my favour.'

She set about her chores in the kitchen while Jayden sat at the table, happily sticking tissue and coloured paper shapes to small pieces of card.

'Look what I did,' he said, after a while. 'It's a card for Mummy.'

'Let me see.' She looked at the collection of white tissue-paper flowers he'd carefully stuck down onto a folded piece of blue card. 'Well, that's just lovely,' she told him. 'Shall we put a yellow middle on the flower?'

He nodded eagerly. 'She likes daisies,' he said.

'Good. I'm sure she'll love it. You can give it to her when we go to the hospital next time.'

'Yeah. I've putted lots of kisses, see?'

'Oh, yes.' She smiled. Half the page was filled with pencilled crosses.

He finished off the card and a little while later she sent him to the bathroom to get ready for bed while she made him a drink of hot chocolate.

'I'm not tired,' he complained, as she tucked the bedcovers around him a few minutes later. 'I don't go to bed this early...ever.' Again, there was that wide-eyed look of innocence that she was coming to recognise.

'Well, you don't have to go to sleep. We'll just look at the storybook together for a while, shall we?' And as usual he fell asleep within minutes.

Leaving his door slightly ajar, she went quietly downstairs and started to tidy up.

The doorbell sounded as she finished washing dishes and she went to answer it, wondering who would be calling on her at this time of the evening.

'I hope you don't mind?' James said, giving her a quizzical look. 'I've just finished work at the hospital and was passing by on my way home. I thought it might be good if we could talk.'

She opened the door for him to enter. 'You'd better come in.'

She showed him into the sitting room. 'Have a seat,' she said, whisking a couple of toy cars from the settee and waving him to the space she'd cleared.

James glanced around the homely room and then sat down. 'I suppose Jayden must be in bed by now?'

She nodded. 'He always complains that he has to go to bed too early, and yet he's asleep within minutes every time.' All the time she was talking she was busy scooping up magazines and a newspaper, which she dropped carefully into a wooden rack.

'I guess you have your hands full, with work at the hospital, your TV programmes and looking after a child, as well.' James watched her as she moved around the room. 'You do all this on your own?'

'I'm sure lots of women do it all the time.' She picked up a cushion and plumped it up just so that she could keep busy...anything rather than sit down and talk to him face to face.

'I expect so.' He hesitated, and then asked, 'Might I ask—is his father around?'

'He's in Switzerland, sorting out some major

problems with his business—financial troubles and difficulties with the workforce, that sort of thing. He's managed to get back a few times over the last couple of weeks.'

'Oh, I see.'

'I don't think you do.' She stopped tidying up and came to sit opposite him, in one of the arm-chairs. 'Jayden is my neighbour's little boy. She's in hospital, suffering from pre-eclampsia.'

'Ah.' He gave a rueful smile. 'I had it all wrong. That will teach me not to jump to conclusions.'

'Maybe.'

'How's it going with the boy? Are you coping all right?'

'I'm not sure. I think so—he seems happy enough, though he's upset about his mother having a baby. He thinks she should give it away.'

He laughed. 'Well, that's not good.'

'No.' She was silent for a moment then said, 'Actually, I've been racking my brains for a way around the problem. I don't like to see him upset, and his mother has enough to contend with right now.'

'Hmm.' He thought for a while. 'I suppose there must be storybooks about children having to face up to a new child in the family. There must be one out there that will help him see the situation in a new light.'

She exhaled as though a small weight had been lifted from her. 'You're right. Why didn't I think of that? I'll go along to the bookshop and see if I can find one or two.' She sent him a quick glance, beginning to feel a little better about having him there.

'Was there a reason you came to see me?' she asked.

He nodded. 'I realise I upset you earlier today, and I wanted to apologise for that. You were quite right. I was out of order. How you and Lewis relate to one another is none of my business.'

She thought about it. 'Perhaps I was a bit touchy,' she conceded. 'With one thing and another—Mel taking the complaint further, and work, and the stress of working on a TV series—it's possible I could have overreacted.' Now that she'd had time to get a grip on herself she was beginning to regret her quick flare of annoyance. Perhaps she'd taken on too much and it was showing in the way she reacted to situations.

'We're okay, then?' He stood up and went over to her. 'I wouldn't like to think that things are strained between us.'

She nodded, getting to her feet. 'That would be awkward, seeing that we have to work together, wouldn't it?'

'It would.' He laid his hands gently around her arms, his long fingers making bands of heat on her bare skin. 'I'd much rather we had a good working relationship.' He smiled. 'In fact, we'll probably be working together more than you think.'

'Oh? How is that?' His touch was doing strange things to her nervous system. She was finding it more and more difficult to concentrate.

'I have to go to the TV studios on Saturday,' he answered. 'I'm going to record a programme about the Birchenall history—didn't you mention that you were going to the studios that day, too?'

'That's right.' She looked at him curiously, and as she moved slightly, he drew her into the circle of his arms. 'How did it come about that you're doing a show—didn't you say you hadn't time to do that sort of thing?' His nearness was disconcerting. At the same time he was so near, it seemed, and yet so far away. She was beginning to yearn for something much more intimate.

'I did say that.' He half smiled. 'Obviously I spoke too soon, but my father's keen for me to do it. He's very proud of his heritage—though he doesn't often allow the cameras into his home.' His grey gaze moved over her, warming her with its shimmering heat.

Perhaps he, too, was finding their closeness distracting, because all of a sudden he appeared to have trouble thinking straight. 'I think the skirmish with the press made him realise he has to work on his image, so when this opportunity came up, he asked me to stand in for him.' His hand wandered along the length of her spine, coming to rest in the small of her back. 'I want to put his mind at ease, so I agreed.' He drew her closer and the breath caught in her throat as the softness of her curves collided with his toned masculine frame.

'I get the feeling the weight of the Birchenall dynasty lies squarely on your shoulders.'

'Oh, yes.' Again, there was that rueful quirk to his mouth. 'My father is determined that we live up to our heritage.'

'I guess it means everything to him,' she murmured.

'Yes, it does.' He looked down at her, his glance sliding over her flushed face and coming to dwell on the ripe fullness of her lips. All the time his hands gently stroked her, smoothing over the rounded swell of her hips, and her heart began to thump heavily in her chest so that she could feel it banging against her rib cage.

This was much more than a friendly, soothing touch. It was a caress, gossamer-light and incredibly compelling, enticing her to move into the shelter of his strong, male body.

He bent his head towards her, and she realised

what was about to happen. It was as though everything was in slow motion.

'Ellie?'

She didn't know if it was a sigh or a question, the way he said her name. Either way, there was plenty of time for her to make a move, to stop him there and then, but recklessly she did nothing.

'I can't think straight,' he said huskily. 'You've bewitched me.'

She was mesmerised by his warm, comforting presence, and more than anything right now she wanted him to sweep her into his arms and make her troubles fade away.

He didn't let her down. His lips softly claimed her mouth, brushing over it with tender expertise and tantalising her with his coaxing, possessive kiss. Her hands slid upwards, over the flat plane of his stomach and onto his hard rib cage.

He groaned softly and crushed her to him as he deepened the kiss, and she clung to him, her fingertips tracing the line of his powerful biceps. There was strength and control there, arms that could hold a woman fast and promise her heaven on earth.

'You taste so good.' He murmured the words against her lips, and a quick, unexpected ripple of desire flowed through her, shocking her to the core. She'd never felt this way before, never had such a deep-seated longing overwhelm her and cast her inhibitions to the wind.

'Ellie, I want you. I could make life so sweet for you. Give you so much.'

'You don't have to give me anything,' she murmured. She revelled in the way his hands moved over her, shaping her, enticing her to lean into him, to feel her soft body melding with his hard frame.

He kissed her again, a fervent, passionate kiss that stirred her senses and had her almost begging him for more, much more.

'You don't need to be with my cousin,' he said raggedly. 'He's not right for you—let me be the one to make you happy.'

Ellie froze in shock. What was he saying? How could he say those things to her? Did he truly believe she was making a play for Lewis? Was that why he was holding her, kissing her? Just so that he might divert her away from him? Was that what he planned all along?

She stared at him, scarcely able to believe what was happening.

He frowned, conscious of her sudden withdrawal, but when he might have coaxed and cajoled her once more, his phone began to ring. He stood very still for a few seconds while the ringtone burbled. Then, as if he had been woken from a trance, he said quietly, 'I'm sorry about this. I have to answer it. It might be… Excuse me.'

He answered the call. He listened for a moment and then said, 'Sophie, what's wrong? No, I'm at Ellie's house. Yes, I told you about her. We work together.'

He broke off again as Sophie began to speak. Then, 'It's just a few minutes away. Why?'

Sophie answered him and after a short time he interrupted her quickly to say, 'It's all right, I'll come home. Loosen any clothing around his neck and prop him up with pillows. Has he had his glyceryl trinitrate spray?'

He shut off the phone a second or two later and Ellie looked at him worriedly. 'Your father? Do you need an ambulance?' Her mind was a whirl of confusion.

James frowned. 'I'm hoping we can get through this without sending him to hospital— he hates being there. But he went out to visit friends today and now he's having a bad episode. Can't get his breath. It's lucky that Sophie was with him—she has a key to the house so that she can come and go and keep an eye on him for me.' He sucked in a quick breath. 'I'll try him with a stronger diuretic to see if that will help reduce the load on his lungs.'

She went with him to the door. 'Is there any-thing I can do to help?'

He shook his head. 'I have everything I need. Thanks.' He glanced at her briefly. 'Ellie, about you and I. You need to know—'

'Go to your father, James,' she cut in. 'He needs you.'

He drove away and she went back inside the house. She couldn't get her head around what had just happened between them. What had she been thinking of, falling for him that way, when all the time he had been leading her down a false trail?

CHAPTER FIVE

'I WANTED TO wish you good luck, Ellie. I hope the filming goes well for you today.' Lewis was cheerful on the phone, and Ellie smiled.

'Thanks. I've looked through my notes and checked with the studio that all the props are in place, so hopefully it will all go smoothly.'

'It'll be great. I always enjoy watching your shows.'

'I'm glad—though I think you're a teeny bit biased, Lewis!'

'Yeah, maybe.' He chuckled. 'Anyway, I'll let you get off. I know you have to be there a couple of hours beforehand to get your make-up done and so on. I suspect that's why you took the job, so that you could be cosseted every now and again.'

She laughed. 'And why not?'

She finished the call a short time later and went out to the courtyard to say goodbye to Jayden. He was with his grandmother, getting ready to go to his grandparents' house, and she wanted to give back a couple of toys that he had left behind.

'I think you forgot your jigsaw puzzles and the new storybooks,' she said, handing them over.

'Thanks.' He looked in the bag and passed it to his grandmother. 'We're going to see Mummy at the hospital this afternoon,' he said. He frowned. 'I think the baby's coming today.'

'Really? You'll be a big brother—imagine that! It's very important, being a big brother, you know.' Ellie smiled at him and he nodded cautiously.

'Yeah. Mummy said that.'

Ellie looked at his grandmother. She was in her early fifties, a slender woman with neat brown hair feathered around her face. 'He's been a joy to have around,' Ellie told her. 'I shall miss him.'

'We're really grateful to you for looking after him. Thank you so much.'

'You're welcome. If you have any problems and need to have him sleep over any time, just let me know.'

She watched them get into their car and waved as they drove away. Then she slid into her own vehicle and set off for the studios.

The road passed through wooded hills and vales, by gentle waterways, and in the distance she could just about make out the misty peaks of the Pennines. The countryside was beautiful, serene, and incredibly peaceful.

The only blot on her landscape was that James was going to be at the television studios and she hadn't worked out quite how she was going to avoid him. It could be managed, though, because they would be using different studios for their recordings.

Whatever happened, she'd made up her mind that she wasn't going to let him get to her. How could she have been such a fool as to let him work his way into her heart like that, only to have him turn the knife when she least expected it? And why had she even thought about getting together with him when it was clear he wasn't averse to playing around? Wasn't he just like her ex?

Well, it was enough. She'd learned a lesson. He wouldn't get the chance to hurt her again.

Soon the scenery changed from rural to urban, and a few minutes later she slowed the car as she approached the impressive building where the show was to be filmed.

Everything looked spacious, with architect-designed buildings made up of brick and marble and a huge expanse of plate glass, all surrounded by landscaped terraces.

'It's good to see you again, Ellie,' the receptionist said as she walked into the grand foyer. 'They're ready for you in Make-up—you can go straight through.'

'Thanks.'

She drank coffee and chatted while the hairdresser styled her hair, teasing her silky curls into a loose topknot, and then she relaxed while the make-up girl, Alice, set to work, giving her a light touch of foundation and adding a gentle sweep of blusher to her cheeks. At least, she tried to relax.

'I was watching James Birchenall in the garden studio a little earlier,' Alice confided. 'I couldn't resist listening in on his interview. They're going to do some more filming at the house and then piece everything together, but today he was talking about how the land passed to his family in the sixteenth century, and telling us about the gentry who have lived there over the years. Of course the house has been altered in that time, with bits added on here and there.' She sighed. 'How the other half live! I certainly wouldn't mind being *his* other half.'

Ellie chuckled. 'I expect a lot of women feel that way.' Excluding herself, of course. She was immune to him now, wasn't she? But from the sound of things she could rest easy because his programme was over and done with and he was most likely on the road home by now.

After Alice finished working on her make-up the hairdresser came along to add a few finishing touches to her style, and then Ellie went off to record the programme.

She talked about cardiovascular health and how people could look after themselves by eating the right kind of food and getting enough exercise. Then she talked to a nutritionist about fruit and vegetables and cereals, and measured people's blood pressure after cycling and various kinds of exercise.

The programme finally came to an end, and Ellie collected her bag and jacket, ready for the journey home.

'Oh, you mustn't go just yet!' the producer exclaimed. 'I'd like to talk to you about doing another series. I was thinking maybe something on pregnancy and women's health—what do you think?'

She nodded. 'Sounds good. I'd need to expand my list of experts who could take part—but I could ask my friend and colleague Lewis about that.'

'That's great,' he said. 'Look, why don't I join you in the Green Room in half an hour or so and we can talk about it some more? We've laid on quite a spread in there, so you must sample it while you're waiting. There are some prime cuts of meat and great desserts.' He lowered his voice, speaking in a confidential tone. 'You'll have to forget about all the stuff you were saying in your programme just now and live a little, but with your figure it won't hurt, will it?'

She laughed. 'I suppose, if you're going to twist my arm…'

'That's my girl.' He waved her towards the door. 'You won't regret it.'

She went to the Green Room and took advantage of the free time to make a quick call to Lewis.

She told him what the producer had suggested, and asked him about people who might agree to appear on the show.

'That's great news, Ellie,' he said. 'I can think of a few people offhand, who might like to take part. I'll drop by your house one evening— maybe Friday, because Jessica will be out then.

We can talk about it and I'll let you have a list of names.'

'Thanks, Lewis.'

When the call ended, she went to help herself to the buffet, filling her plate with thin slices of roast beef and a generous helping of rice and salad.

'Ellie—I hoped I would see you here today.' James's deep voice smoothed over her, and she looked around to see that he was right by her side.

Hot colour swept along her cheekbones. She'd been congratulating herself on managing to steer clear of him so far, and now he'd turned up when she was trapped with absolutely no excuse to rush away.

'I was rather hoping the opposite,' she murmured.

'You're angry with me?'

'How did you guess?'

His plate was filled with a selection of meats and savoury pastries, she noticed. He had a healthy appetite and never seemed to put on an ounce of fat, and she guessed he burned it up by being constantly on the go.

A waiter offered a selection of wines and fruit juices and she chose a small glass of Bordeaux, as she would be driving later.

She went to sit at a table by the window, over-looking one of the terraces. There were orna-mental cherry trees out there, graceful weeping willows and banks of flowers, and every now and again benches were placed where people could sit for a while and relax. She studied the view for a while, trying unsuccessfully to ignore the fact that James had come to sit opposite her. She was way too conscious of him.

'I don't want to see Lewis getting into some-thing he can't handle,' James said, offering her a bread roll from a wicker basket. 'But that doesn't mean I blame you for anything. I meant what I said to you. You're a beautiful, caring, thought-ful woman. What man wouldn't want to be with you? What would be the harm in you and I get-ting together?'

She could have mentioned his girlfriend—the

woman who spent so much time at the manor house and who, according to Noah, had been singled out for him, coming from a well-to-do family that had been linked to his in friendship for many years. But James was clearly pushing any such thoughts to one side for the time being. Wasn't that what she might have expected, given the way men went from one woman to another, at least in her experience?

Instead, she murmured, 'I can think of a few things offhand.' She speared a cucumber slice and then recounted the list of reasons. 'Let's see; you're devious, conniving, an opportunist—and as you pointed out, should I be foolish enough to be caught out a second time, the rumour mill will start to work overtime at the hospital.'

'We can overcome all those things,' he said. 'They're nothing.'

'Hmm. You would say that, wouldn't you?' She savoured her wine, letting it rest on her tongue for a second or two. 'Of course, there's always the fact that your father hates me.'

'He doesn't. Anyway, my father isn't the one

who wants to date you,' he said, his mouth making an amused quirk.

'That's definitely true.'

She glanced across the room and James must have caught her look of surprise because he turned to follow her gaze and said in a low voice, 'Well, there's a turn-up for the book. What's my father doing here with Sophie?' He frowned. 'I warned him there's no way he should be here.'

'That's what I was thinking,' she said in a puzzled tone. 'I wouldn't have thought he was well enough to be out and about—it was only the other night you had to rush off to help him.'

James nodded. 'I don't know what he can be thinking.'

He stood up. 'Excuse me. I'd better go and invite them over, if that's all right with you?'

'Be my guest,' she said.

It was probably a good thing that she was no longer going to be alone with him. She wouldn't put it past him to wheedle her into believing that she was mistaken in everything she knew about him and that he was actually a saint. Of course he hadn't wanted to prise her away from Lewis. That would have been the furthest thing from his mind. Yeah, right. She had deluded herself into thinking he really wanted her and instead it had simply been a ruse.

Lord Birchenall walked slowly towards her. 'May we sit here?' he asked, and she nodded.

'Please, do.'

'Are you sure we won't be intruding?'

'Not at all. I'll have to leave soon anyway, to go and talk to one of the producers.'

'Thank you.' It was clear that walking had taken the stuffing out of him. She heard the breath wheeze in his lungs, and he paused for a moment to gather strength before saying, 'This is Sophie. She's the daughter of a family friend. She was kind enough to bring me here today.'

'Hello, Sophie.' Ellie tried a smile. Okay, so she might be James's girlfriend, but that didn't matter to her any more, did it? Her stomach churned at the lie, but she had to accept that James was no longer on her radar and, besides, wouldn't Sophie be upset to know that he had been kissing another woman? Another reason why Ellie had to steer clear of him. What kind of man was he who could do that?

Sophie nodded acknowledgement, her gaze moving over Ellie from head to toe. Ellie had the feeling she was being thoroughly assessed. Thank heaven she'd dressed carefully that morning, in a cream-coloured skirt with a matching jacket that nipped in at the waist to flatter her figure. Beneath the jacket she wore a pretty, lace-trimmed top.

Sophie was truly beautiful, a slender girl with honey-gold hair held loosely with a clip at the back. She had deep blue eyes, a perfect, oval face and a full, rose-pink mouth. No wonder James had chosen her.

Sophie sat down, and once she was settled, Lord Birchenall took his seat next to her.

'Would you like something to eat?' Ellie enquired, turning her attention to James's father. 'I could get something for you.'

He shook his head. 'Not for me, thank you. I'll just have a drink. A coffee, perhaps.'

'I'll get it for you,' James said. He stood for a moment by his father's chair. 'It's good to see you, but I can't think what possessed you to come here today. You know I warned you that it might be too much for you.'

'Yes, but…' Lord Birchenall paused, his breath coming in short gasps. 'I wanted to watch the recording. After all, it was our heritage that you were talking about.'

James patted his shoulder. 'I know how much it means to you, but I don't want to see you struggling. I could have shown you the recording later.'

His father smiled. 'Ah, yes, but it wouldn't have been quite the same. And Sophie offered to bring me, so I jumped at the chance.'

'And was it worth it?'

'Oh, yes. It will be a good programme.'

'I'm glad you think so.' James smiled and went to fetch food and drink for Sophie and his father, leaving Ellie to chat with them for a while.

'Did you enjoy the show, Sophie?' she asked.

'I did. I thought James was wonderful and

he chose the best video footage that shows the manor in all its glory.' Her gaze drifted over Ellie once more. 'I take it James invited you to come and watch the show?'

Ellie shook her head. 'Actually, no. I came here to make a recording of my own. I do a medical programme that's airing once a week at the moment. Perhaps you've heard of it—it's called *Your Good Health*?'

'No, I'm afraid not.'

Lord Birchenall was intrigued, his face lighting up with recognition. 'So that's it. I thought I knew you from somewhere, other than when you lived at the lodge. I watch that series. You should be pleased with yourself. It's very well done.'

'Thank you.' She was surprised he was being so generous, given the way he'd reacted to her when she'd visited the house, but perhaps James was right when he'd said the shock of the newspaper article had made his father more tetchy than usual. 'I can't take the credit, though—there's a whole team who helps put it together.'

She sipped her wine and glanced at him once more. He seemed to be breathing a bit better now that he was sitting down. 'Have you fully recovered from your upset the other day? It sounded as though you were very ill.'

'I'm much better, thank you. It's a sad fact that my health is not good these days, but I'm fortunate in having James to watch over me.'

James came back just then with a plate of food for Sophie and two coffees.

Sophie was deep in thought. 'Is it right, that you lived at the lodge?' she asked, turning to Ellie.

Ellie nodded, and Sophie reclined back in her seat. 'Of course,' she said. 'I remember hearing something about that. Your father worked for Lord Birchenall, but he left, didn't he?'

Lord Birchenall gave her a sharp look and shifted uneasily in his seat. 'Ahem,' he said, but Sophie ploughed on.

'Wasn't there some sort of problem?'

Once again, Lord Birchenall tried to intervene.

'I don't think we need to go into that,' he said. 'It was all a long time ago.'

'Oh, but—' Sophie continued, and this time James interrupted.

'As my father said, Sophie, I don't think we want to delve into the past. Ellie's worked hard to make a career for herself. She works in A and E, as well as doing a TV series.'

'Really. How interesting.' She frowned and looked at Ellie once more. 'You've done well for yourself, haven't you, considering your troubles over the years? I heard a little about the family who lived in the lodge.'

'As James said, I've worked hard to overcome all that,' Ellie responded. 'As to my father, we didn't know it at the time, but he was actually quite ill. Later on he had to go into hospital for a few weeks.'

Sophie delicately sliced the meat on her plate. 'I'm sorry to hear that. What was wrong with him?'

'He had Addison's disease. It's an endocrine disorder that makes the patient very ill.'

Lord Birchenall looked shocked. 'I'm so sorry, my dear. I didn't know that.'

She nodded briefly. 'None of us did at first.' Even now it haunted her that she hadn't seen what had been happening to her father, that she hadn't realised he was ill. She'd been angry with Lord Birchenall for the way he'd treated him, but wasn't she just as guilty for not recognising that something was wrong?

She said carefully, 'It's quite rare, and it was some time before his condition was properly diagnosed.'

'I recall you told me something of this last time we met, when you came to the house.' He frowned. 'I'm afraid I wasn't myself that day, what with all that business of our family splashed over the Sunday papers.'

Sophie laid down her fork. 'It was very distressing that you had to go through all that,' she said. 'It's no wonder you weren't yourself.'

Ellie pushed her chair back carefully and stood up. 'If you'll excuse me,' she said, 'I can see my producer's just arrived. I'd better go and join him.'

James stood up with her. 'I'm glad we met up today,' he said, moving with her away from the table. He laid his arm lightly beneath her elbow. 'You mustn't take any notice of Sophie. She doesn't always think before she speaks. She's one of these people who say what's on their minds without considering the effect on other people.'

'Like your father said, it was all a long time ago.'

'How is your father these days? Is the disease under control?'

'I believe so. Of course, if he gets an infection or if he's stressed, his symptoms flare up and he becomes very tired and doesn't cope so well. When I spoke to him last week, he was feeling fine.'

They'd almost reached the bar, where her producer was ordering a drink, and Ellie stood still, ready to part company with James.

'Do you ever think about making a new start

with your mother?' he asked. 'After all, you said she was in hospital for a time. Perhaps her illness affected her and made her distant and unable to cope.'

'It's possible, I suppose, though I think you're being ultra-kind about her. She chose to leave us, after all. I'm afraid I'm not like you. I find it hard to be generous in those circumstances.'

He lightly ran his hand over her arm. 'It's understandable. I don't know how I would have reacted in that situation.' He smiled. 'The same way you did, probably.'

She thought about the way she had responded when her mother had gone away. Over the next few years she'd turned to drink and wild parties in town that had sometimes spilled out onto the street. Her picture had ended up in the local paper when the rowdiness had annoyed the nearby residents. She gave him a wry smile. 'And risk bringing your family into disrepute?' She shook her head. 'I don't think so somehow.'

'Oh, I don't know. I think I'd quite like the opportunity to be disreputable with you,' he said, amusement glimmering in the depths of his eyes.

'Chance would be a fine thing,' she murmured. 'Anyway, I think you have other obligations right now.' She glanced at the table by the window where Sophie and his father were chatting.

Every now and again Sophie would shoot a look in their direction, and Ellie began to feel uncomfortable. Whatever James's feelings might be, Sophie was definitely interested in him.

He followed her gaze. 'You're right,' he agreed, bracing his shoulders. 'I just felt that I needed to put your mind at rest over Sophie. She's very forthright, but she's not bad at heart. She genuinely doesn't realise she might be upsetting people.'

'No, but she might be quite upset if you don't go and join her at the table very soon,' she said.

He nodded. 'Maybe I'll see you later?' he suggested.

'Possibly.' But she knew she wouldn't. As soon as she'd finished talking to her producer, she would slip away and drive home. She needed to put some space between herself and the Birchenalls...and Sophie.

CHAPTER SIX

ELLIE DROPPED THE letter into the wire tray. So the second meeting with Amelia Holt was to take place in another six weeks' time. Six more weeks of waiting to find out if her career was going to be safe.

She hadn't voiced her thoughts out loud, but James must have guessed what she was thinking.

'Don't let it get to you,' he said. 'No sensible person could see her getting anywhere with such a complaint. She's just not thinking straight. Losing her aunt must have shaken her really badly and turned her mind.'

'Perhaps you're right.' She gave a rueful smile. 'Maybe she'll come to her senses before too long.'

'I'm sure she will.'

But that wouldn't happen any time soon, Ellie

reflected, if the email she'd received from Mel that morning was anything to go by. She wasn't going to tell James about it. *'Why don't you face up to things and accept you were in the wrong? Why prolong the inevitable for another six weeks?'* Mel must have been informed of the date of the next meeting at the same time she had been.

The phone rang in A and E and Olivia went to answer it. 'There's an emergency coming in,' she said. 'It's a woman complaining of chest pains and difficulty breathing.'

'Okay. Room Two is free, so I'll see her in there as soon as she comes in.' Ellie left James to go and look after his own patients and went to make preparations. Then she hurried down to the ambulance bay to receive her patient.

The woman was very distressed and fearful, and Ellie hurried to reassure her. 'We'll take good care of you, Angela,' she said, checking her name from the notes. 'I'll take you in to the examination room and then we'll do what we can to make you feel more comfortable.'

'Thank you.' Angela struggled to say the words, exhausted by her struggle to get air into her lungs, and Ellie could see that she was gravely ill.

When they were in the treatment room, she gave her oxygen through a mask to help her breathing and gently questioned her about the events leading to her illness.

'I had a…chest infection,' Angela said in a halting voice, moving the oxygen mask briefly away from her face. 'Everything feels…so tight in my chest. It's such a…sharp, stabbing pain. It feels really…bad.'

'Perhaps you'll feel a bit better if we sit you up,' Ellie said, noticing how the woman tried to lean forward to relieve the pain. She raised the bed head while Olivia brought more pillows to prop her up, and Angela gave a small sigh of relief as she sank back against them.

Ellie examined her, and became increasingly worried. 'You're feverish,' she said. 'I'm going to order some blood tests and a CT scan so that we can find out what's going on in your chest.

In the meantime, I'll give you a painkiller and start you on antibiotics, because I suspect you have a nasty infection.'

Angela nodded, restless with pain and discomfort, too ill to say much more, and Ellie set about preparing the injection.

She was writing out the lab forms when James came into the room a little later. 'Is everything all right in here?'

He introduced himself to the patient, putting her at ease, and then moved away from the bedside so that he could talk to Ellie.

'How's it going?' he asked, and she turned away so that the woman wouldn't see or hear what she said.

'I've examined her, and the heart sounds are very faint. There's a rubbing sound, too, and I think there's fluid in the pericardium and around her lungs.'

'So you're thinking...?'

'Pericarditis.' Her heart began to thump heavily as she said it. 'The same as Grace Holt,' she added, 'though maybe with a different cause.'

Memories rushed to fill her mind, and all at once she was starting to feel shaky inside and chills were shooting up and down her spine.

She knew the colour had drained from her face. Was she up to dealing with this? Had she gone wrong before somehow when she'd treated Mel's aunt? Was she to go through it all again and finish with the same outcome?

James studied her pale features, his dark eyes giving nothing away, but she knew he must be weighing up her response to the situation. 'You're doing tests?'

She nodded. 'It'll be a while before we get the results from the lab, but I'll do a scan and go from there. I have her on anti-inflammatory medication and diuretics to reduce the fluid volume.'

'Okay. Let me know as soon as you hear.'

'I will.'

He touched her arm briefly as he left the room, and that small act of encouragement helped her to feel a tiny bit better. She wasn't alone, he was silently telling her, and she was grateful for his support. Even so, she was worried sick.

The CT films made her even more anxious when she brought them up on screen some time later. She'd been right about the fluid around the heart and lungs. This was beginning to look exactly like Grace Holt's illness.

'I've looked at your scan,' she told Angela, 'but we're going to do another test, an echocardiogram, so that we can see how your heart is working. It's nothing to worry about and it's a painless procedure—the technician will glide a device over your chest and a picture will come up on the monitor.'

James came to look at the films with her later on when some of the lab reports had also come through.

'You were right,' he said. 'It is an inflammation around the heart. The infection is stopping the heart from pumping properly. We need to prep her for a pericardiocentesis.' He sent her a quick glance. 'Are you okay with that?'

'Yes.' She wasn't, but she had to prove to herself that she could do it, and for Angela's sake they had to drain the fluid from around her heart as quickly as possible. It would have been more usual for James to take over at this point, being the senior doctor, but she guessed he saw this as a way of getting her to face her demons. 'I'll get the equipment ready.'

He helped her to prepare the patient for the procedure, and when they were finally ready, and Angela had been given a local anaesthetic, Ellie ran the ultrasound probe over her chest, glancing at the computer screen to make sure she had the right location.

'I'm going in through the fifth intercostal space,' she said, checking the point of entry between the ribs. Then she inserted a long spinal needle into Angela's chest, checking to see that the woman was coping with the procedure.

Ellie had to take the utmost care to avoid puncturing vital organs and arteries, and she positioned the needle carefully so that it entered the pericardial space around the heart. She could see it all on the screen. 'Are you all right, Angela?' she asked again.

The woman nodded and slowly Ellie began to draw off fluid into the syringe.

'Her vital signs are improving a little,' James said. To Angela, he commented, 'You should start to feel more comfortable as the pressure eases off your heart.'

Ellie handed him the filled syringe and exchanged it for a new one.

'We'll send that for analysis,' James said, and added in a low voice, 'You're doing great. Keep going.'

She nodded, glad of his encouragement. A faint film of perspiration dampened her brow and James said quietly, 'I'll wipe that for you.' He gently dabbed her forehead with a cloth.

'Thanks.' When she had drained as much fluid as possible, she put a catheter in place and connected a drainage tube and bag.

'How does that feel?' she asked her patient.

'It's so much better,' Angela said, sounding exhausted. 'It's such a relief not to feel that pressure and that awful pain.'

'I'm glad.' Ellie was thankful that everything had gone without complication. Angela wasn't out of the woods yet, though. The infection that had caused the build-up of fluid was still active, and the antibiotics needed time to work. In Grace Holt's case, the infection had proved overwhelming, and she had died of a sudden heart attack.

Ellie left the woman in the care of a nurse and walked back to the main desk to check her list of patients.

'I think you deserve a break,' James said, getting into step alongside her. 'You haven't stopped since first thing this morning. Let's go and get some lunch.'

'Okay. That sounds like a good idea.' Perhaps she ought not to spend time with him, but it was hard for her to put up any resistance. Whenever she was near him she found herself wanting to prolong that contact.

They went to the restaurant, where they filled

their trays with a selection of food from the chilled cabinets.

'It's warm today,' James said. 'Shall we go and sit outside?'

'Perfect.' She chose a bench table close by a spreading old beech tree. Its trunk was wide and its branches were thick and long, and sunlight filtered through the leaves. There were tables dotted around at intervals on the grass, but they were all deserted, and she guessed this was because it was well past the usual time for lunch.

James smiled at her as he started on his chicken salad. 'You did well back there. How do you feel?'

'I'm not sure.' She'd been holding her breath for so long, it seemed, and now that she could breathe freely again she was still cautious, anxious in case anything went wrong.

'You did everything right,' he said. 'Just as you did last time. Relax.'

'Yes, I'll try.' She tasted the grated cheese on her plate and washed it down with a chilled fruit juice.

The sun was warm on her bare arms, and gradually, as they talked, her spirits began to lift.

'What's happening with your neighbour?' James asked. 'Didn't you tell me she's had her baby?'

'That's right. Lewis did a Caesarean a couple of days ago. She had a little girl.' She smiled. 'She's a beautiful little thing, all soft, downy skin and curly brown hair. They'll be discharging Lily from hospital later today, provided her blood pressure is stable. I think Lewis plans to keep her there most of the day, just to be certain she's all right. Anyway, I said I would look after Jayden while her husband goes to fetch them from the hospital. I think they're planning on stopping by her sister's house to show her the baby.'

'Aren't the grandparents around to look after Jayden?'

'Not today, unfortunately. His grandfather has gone down with some kind of stomach bug and they're steering clear so as not to infect anybody.'

'That's bad luck.' He looked at her curiously. 'You don't seem to mind looking after him.'

'No, I don't, although it can be a bit tiring, because four-year-olds don't have an off button and they just never seem to stop.' She chuckled. 'He's very easy to entertain, though.' She mused on that for a while. 'I think we might do some baking this evening. He likes doing that, and I expect Lily and her husband will enjoy eating the cakes afterwards.'

'I'm sure they will.' His dark gaze wandered over her. 'Have you ever thought about having a family of your own?'

She pondered on that for a while. 'Yes, I have.' She returned his glance fleetingly. Until now, she'd never met a man she would want as the father of her children, but James was different from anyone she'd ever met. He was extra-special, and she could definitely see him in that role. A small ripple of awareness ran through her, and she had to pull herself together and answer his question properly as he was looking at her expectantly.

'As far as my mother is concerned, I don't have a great example of parenting to work from but that just makes me want to make up for it with my own family. I definitely want to have children at some point.'

Her gaze met his once more. 'What about you? I expect your father hopes you'll have a son one day to continue the line.' Her mouth curved. 'How do you feel about that?'

He gave a soft laugh. 'Oh, yes, there is that. But putting my father's wishes to one side, I'd like a family of my own one day.'

He pushed his plate away and started on his dessert, a cream-topped strawberry trifle. His expression became serious. 'Have you thought any more about visiting your mother? From the way you reacted to my father in the beginning, I sense there's a lot of pent-up emotion stemming from your teenage years. Perhaps it would do you both the world of good to talk things through.'

She shook her head. 'Perhaps, some time in the future, I might seek her out. The way I feel at the moment, though, is that she chose to leave and for any reconciliation to be meaningful she should be the one to make the first move.' A small tremor of unease ran through her. Was she being fair to her mother in thinking this way? Hadn't her mother had problems to overcome, too?

He nodded. 'I suppose I can see the logic behind that.'

They talked for a while longer but then their pagers began to bleep simultaneously, a warning of another emergency patient coming in.

'Hey-ho,' James said. 'Off we go again.'

Ellie looked after her patients through the course of the day, and just before her shift was due to end she went to check on Angela. The drainage tube and bag were filling up, showing signs that the infection was still raging, but she wasn't as breathless as she had been earlier, and though her heart rate and blood pressure were still giving cause for concern, her condition was relatively stable for now.

Ellie went home and picked up Jayden from

her neighbour's house, but she didn't stop to chat for long because Lewis had said he was going to drop by later on and she needed to get organised. She wasn't expecting Lily to be home for a few hours yet.

'So what do you think of your new sister?' she asked Jayden when they were home.

He wriggled his shoulders. 'She's all right, I suppose. She doesn't do anything, though, except sleep and yawn, and sometimes she cries.'

Ellie nodded. 'Babies do quite a lot of that,' she said. 'It's their way of letting us know they need something.'

She changed out of her work clothes into jeans and a top, and after they had eaten she showed him the cookery book and let him choose what they were going to make.

'Cupcakes,' he said, his eyes growing round as he looked at the pictures. 'Those with the pink stuff on top.'

'Hmm. Pink for a girl. That seems about right.'

Just over an hour later she set the cakes out on a tiered cake stand and they inspected the finished results. 'They look pretty good, don't they?'

Jayden nodded. 'Can I have one now?'

'Of course you can. I think you've earned it after all that work.'

The doorbell rang and she went to greet Lewis. Jayden came with her to see who was there, and looked disappointed for a second or two when he realised it wasn't his mother. He held onto Ellie's jeans and she put an arm around his shoulders, recognising that he was shy of strangers.

'Lewis,' she said, 'I wasn't sure if you would remember. It's good to see you.'

'And you.' He gently touched her arm and while she appreciated the tender gesture of affection she felt a momentary quiver of unease. Could James have been right when he'd said Lewis wanted more than friendship from her? Surely not?

'I wouldn't forget,' he said. 'Sophie invited my wife to some sort of women's fashion evening, so I told her I'd come to see you and drop off that list of names you wanted for the TV series.'

'Oh, you have it with you? That's great,' she said. 'Thanks.' She shook off her worries about him. Lewis had never given her any reason for concern.

He smiled at Jayden. 'Hello, young man. I don't think we've met before, have we?'

Jayden shook his head. 'I'm Jayden,' he said. 'Who are you?'

Lewis chuckled. 'I'm a friend of Ellie's,' he said. 'I've come to talk over a few things with her.'

'Okay.'

They went into the living room, and Ellie settled Jayden down with some paper and crayons. Once he was busy drawing, Lewis suggested that they sit down and talk about the experts on his list.

'I've made a few notes about each one and where they might fit in with your kind of programme,' he said. 'For instance, there's a doctor who knows all about scans and how to interpret the images, and another who could talk about gestational diabetes.'

'That sounds good.' They went through the list and talked about how the programmes might take form.

'Thanks for this, Lewis,' she said after a while. 'It'll be a great help when we come to set up the series.'

'You're welcome. I'll do whatever I can to help out.' He glanced at his watch. 'I should go. Jessica will be home soon from her fashion thing—'

'All right.' They stood up and Jayden came over to them, thrusting a piece of paper into Ellie's hand.

'It's a car,' he said. 'My car—for when I'm big. It goes really fast.'

She looked down at the drawing. It was a blue streak of a car with a rainbow trail of fumes coming from twin exhaust pipes at the back. She smiled at him. 'It's beautiful, Jayden. Is that you in the driver's seat?'

He nodded, beaming with satisfaction as he walked with Ellie and Lewis to the front door. Ellie glanced at Lewis. 'Between us we've managed to come up with some great ideas for programmes. I can't wait to tell my producer about them.'

'He'll love what you have planned.'

She opened the door, and as they were saying goodbye they were both distracted by the sound of a car door slamming at the end of the drive.

Someone shouted, 'Ellie Saunders? This way, Ellie. Look over here.'

Startled, Ellie looked to where the sound was coming from and saw a man pointing a camera in her direction. All three of them were caught in the flash that followed. The camera whirred a couple more times before she realised what was happening and she quickly ushered Jayden back inside the house. She was completely taken aback by what had just gone on.

'Who is he? What's going on?'

Lewis shook his head. 'I don't know, Ellie, but he looks to me as though he might be someone from the press. Perhaps it's something to do with the TV programme. You're getting to be quite famous after all, a household name.'

'Oh, heavens. What am I to do?'

'Leave it to me. I'll see to it that he goes away,' Lewis told her, his mouth making a grim line. 'You go back inside the house.'

'Are you sure?'

'It'll be fine. Goodbye, Ellie.' He strode down the path and the man must have read the dark intent in his features because he dived into his car and revved the engine before screeching away down the road.

Ellie watched Lewis drive away and then shut the door, leading Jayden back to the kitchen.

He said happily, 'That man took a picture of me.'

'He did, sweetheart. He took a picture of all of us.' She settled him down at the kitchen table and he started eagerly on another picture.

She was jittery, completely unsettled by the intrusion, and for a while she paced the floor. Would he come back? He had what he wanted, after all.

She felt dreadful. The episode had upset her, and she couldn't quite fathom the reason. Perhaps it was fear of the unknown. What was the man intending to do with the photos? What did he want with her?

The doorbell rang for the second time that evening and she jumped nervously. Had he decided to return after all to cause more trouble?

Jayden looked at her. 'Is it the man?'

'I don't know.' She stood up and made an effort to stay calm for Jayden's sake. 'How's your colouring coming along?'

He lifted his book to show her. 'It's a boat on the water, see? And there's a frog sitting on a leaf.'

She nodded and said absently, 'It's called a lily pad. And you've coloured the picture really well.'

The doorbell rang again, sending a small shudder through her. She had to face up to it and go to see who was there. There was more than one kind of demon to be faced, she was discovering.

She was ultra-cautious when she opened the door, and felt a surge of relief when she saw it was James standing there.

He gave her a searching look. 'You're white as a sheet,' he said. 'What's happened? Are you ill?'

'I'm fi—' she began, and he cut in sharply.

'And don't tell me you're fine because I can see quite plainly that you're not.'

'I've had a strange visitor,' she said, opening the door wider and waving James inside. Seeing him standing there had been like the sun breaking through clouds on a dull day. Somehow, with James around, she immediately felt safe, as though nothing else mattered.

'It was just a photographer,' she explained. 'He called my name and started clicking away with his camera. I've no idea what he was doing here, but he took several photos of us.'

'Us?' James echoed.

'Lewis was here.' She led the way to the kitchen and went to the sink to fill the kettle. It gave her something to do and the mundane task was comforting somehow.

James frowned. 'Perhaps it was a good thing he was here with you. It looks as though you've had a bit of a shock.'

She nodded. 'I can't think of any reason for him to turn up here. Lewis thinks it could be something to do with the TV series. He says I'm newsworthy now that I'm getting to be a household name.'

'Could be, I suppose.'

James glanced at Ellie as she busied herself making tea, and she sensed he knew she was staying on the move so as not to give way to her anxieties.

'I came to see if you needed some help with the young lad,' he said, 'but it looks as though you have everything under control.'

She nodded. 'We've had a busy time, haven't we, Jayden? I can't remember how many cakes we made.'

'Lots,' he said, then crinkled his brow. 'This many.' He held up his hands, his fingers spread wide. 'But I had two of them.' He bent two fingers downwards.

'I think we should offer some to James, don't you?'

Jayden frowned, looking first at the cake stand

and then at James. 'Yeah, okay,' he said after a while. He watched anxiously as James picked out a pink-topped cupcake covered in edible silver balls, but looked relieved when he seemed satisfied with just one.

Ellie set about making a pot of tea, and when she turned round she saw that James and Jayden were busy picking out the cakes that had the best decoration.

'That can't be one of yours,' James said, shaking his head. 'It's way too special. You're only... what is it, four years old? You couldn't have done that. Could you?'

'I did! I did it!'

'What, all by yourself?' James put on an incredulous face and Jayden jumped up and down in his seat with delight.

'Yeah, all by myself.'

'Wow!' James laughed and turned to Ellie. 'It sounds as though he's had a great time.'

'I guess he did.' It was heart-warming to see the way James and the little boy interacted.

James clearly had a knack for dealing with young children.

She picked up Jayden's discarded colouring book and pencils and dropped them into his schoolbag. 'There are some toys in the box in the sitting room,' she told the boy. 'Why don't you go and choose something to play with?'

Jayden slid down from his seat at the table and went off to find the box, and Ellie watched as he settled down in a far corner with some construction blocks. Because of the L-shaped design of the house she could still keep an eye on him from the kitchen if she walked over to the worktop.

She poured tea from the pot into two ceramic mugs and passed one to James. 'It was thoughtful of you to come and see me,' she said.

He swallowed some of the hot liquid. 'Well, I know you've had a difficult day, in more ways than one, so I wondered if you might be glad of a helping hand. Like you said, four-year-olds can be wonderful, but exhausting sometimes.'

He placed the mug down on the table and

moved towards her. 'You've a bit more colour in your cheeks now, at any rate.' He slid his arms around her waist. 'I hope that's down to me and not Lewis.'

Much as she liked having his arms around her, her brows drew together in a frown at his comment. 'I thought we'd discussed all that.'

'Did we? I'm not so sure we're both singing from the same song sheet somehow. Lewis is a married man, but he was here, after all. It seems he can't keep away.'

'He was here because he brought me some information for my TV series.' She felt exasperated. 'I don't know why I'm bothering to explain things to you.'

'Maybe it's because you and I both know he could have given you any information you needed at work.'

'But there's absolutely no reason why he shouldn't bring it here.'

'No—except he seems to find it hard to keep away. He needs to be protected from himself.'

She scowled at him. 'I give up. You're impossible. I'm pretty sure Lewis can sort out his own

marital problems without any help from you.'
She tried to wriggle out of his grasp but he only
wound his arms more closely about her.

'But, like I said before, you don't need Lewis
hanging around—you and I could be wonderful
together if you would give us half a chance.' His
hands made gentle forays along the length of her
spine. 'You're like one of those gorgeous cupcakes—perfect in every way, deliciously tempting, and definitely more than I can resist.'

She gave a soft laugh. 'You make them sound
positively sinful.'

'Mmm…that, too,' he murmured, nuzzling the
sensitive flesh behind her ear. 'I could lose myself in you, Ellie.' His lips drifted sensually over
the column of her throat, and as she turned her
head a fraction he swooped to claim her mouth.
Her body tingled as his lips pressured hers, and
his kiss made her blood sizzle, sending ripples
of pleasure surging through her from head to
toe. She was lost in that kiss, swirling in a mist
of heady delight.

'I ache for you, Ellie,' he said, his voice roughened with desire. His hands shaped her, exploring the rounded contours of her body and bringing her up closer to him so that her soft curves meshed with his powerful frame. 'You make me feel so good.'

It was sheer bliss to have him hold her this way, and for a while she felt exhilarated in the delicious sensations that quivered along her nerve endings, yearning for this moment to go on and on.

But with a four-year-old just a short distance away and liable to come into the kitchen at any moment, it would have been madness to go on.

'James, we can't do this,' she said in a low voice. 'Jayden is…'

'I know.' He sighed raggedly. He held her for a few seconds longer before reluctantly easing back. 'I want you all to myself.'

She looked up at him, a bemused expression on her face. She was besieged by a whole array of conflicting emotions, not least of which was where Sophie fitted into any of this.

'What is it?' he asked, giving her a quizzical look.

'You said you want me all to yourself, but aren't you dating Sophie? That's what Noah's article said and Sophie seems to be at the manor house quite often.'

Her question must have caught him unawares because he was serious all at once, and he appeared to be deep in thought. 'Sophie's family has been linked to ours socially for many years,' he said at last. 'Her parents are on very friendly terms with my father.'

'But you've taken her out? That's true, isn't it? You've been out with her recently?'

'Yes, I have.' He frowned. 'The situation with Sophie is complicated. She helps out a lot with my father so I see her quite regularly, and there are social occasions when we meet because of my father's friendship with her parents. But none of that has to affect you and me.'

'Doesn't it? I think you might be wrong there.'

She moved away from him. She wasn't sure he'd given her a straight answer, and as far as she was concerned, that meant he was out of bounds from now on.

'Why, Ellie? You were with me all the way just now. You wanted me every bit as much as I want you. I felt it. So what went wrong?'

'Nothing. You're right, I did want to be in your arms but I came to my senses. I can't get involved with any man who casts his net wide. I've been caught that way before, and I vowed I would never let it happen to me again. I went out with a man for quite a while, and I really liked him, but then I went out with some girl friends and saw him wining and dining another woman. They were holding hands and whispering to one another, and they walked out of that place with their arms around one another.'

He sucked in his breath. 'I'm sorry that happened to you, Ellie. But this isn't the same. It isn't what you think. It's all to do with heritage and family links—all the sort of things my father holds dear. I don't want to cause him any upset while his health is in such a precarious state. But my seeing Sophie doesn't mean anything, believe me. She's just the daughter of a family friend.'

'I wonder if Sophie understands that?'

He frowned. 'She doesn't have anything to do with what's between you and me.'

'No? It doesn't sit well with me, James.'

'Ellie—the truth is, I'm not ready for any sort of commitment yet. I have a lot of responsibility as well as having to look out for my father and overseeing the management of the estate. But I don't see any reason why we can't have fun and enjoy things the way they are.'

'I understand that but I'm not sure I can go along with it.' She frowned. 'I need time to think, so perhaps you should go. I think we've said all we need to say. I was carried away for a moment, but it won't happen again. I wasn't thinking straight.'

'You know I like being with you.'

'And I like being with you, but I'm pretty sure this is not going to work out the way you were perhaps expecting.'

She'd made up her mind, and he must have seen that because he went to say goodbye to Jayden and left the house soon afterwards.

Ellie shut the door behind him and felt a bleak wave of emptiness wash over her. She missed him already.

CHAPTER SEVEN

'ELLIE, WHAT'S GOING on?' Noah sounded really concerned. 'I saw the papers this morning and wanted to talk to you about what I read in there. I've been ringing you for ages but I couldn't get through.'

'It's the press, Noah. They won't leave me alone.' There was a note of desperation in Ellie's voice. 'They've been calling all morning and I stopped answering the phone, until I saw your name on the caller display. I switched off my mobile phone because they even managed to find that number. It's driving me crazy. And it's not just that. They're camped out at the front of the house, too.'

'Have you tried calling the police?'

'Yes, they've moved them on once, but they keep coming back. It's been going on since six o'clock this morning.' She gave a heavy sigh. 'At least they've stopped knocking on the door. I've locked myself in. I don't know what else to do.'

'I suppose you could try speaking to them.'

'And have more rubbish printed about me? I can't do that. It's bad enough that they dragged up all the stuff from my past—they even found pictures from the local newspaper back then. They made me look like the all-time drunken party girl. That headline: *"TV's Ellie Saunders as you have never seen her before."* It made me feel sick.'

'I guessed you must be feeling pretty bad. It must have been a tremendous shock.'

'Yes, it was. But it's Lewis's wife I feel sorry for. They've tried to make out that Lewis and I are having an affair—they even linked Jayden with both of us. Can you believe it? How could they do this?' She frowned. 'It just makes me realise how Lord Birchenall must have felt when the press bombarded him after your story was printed. Until now, I hadn't imagined just how bad it could be.'

'I know. Me, too.' He was contrite. 'I feel terrible about what I did. But I was just so full of
anger at the time. I kept thinking how he threw
us out and the family broke up. All I could think
about was that here was a way of getting back
at him at last, but I'm really sorry for it now.'
He pulled in a quick breath as a thought struck
him. 'Do you think he could be behind all this
stuff in the papers?'

'Surely not? I don't think he would stoop to
something like that. Lewis is his nephew. Whatever he is, he's not vindictive, and even if he
was, I can't see James letting him do something
like this.'

'I guess you're right. So, do you have any idea
who might have gone to the papers?'

'No. I can't think straight. It's been such a
shock.'

'Is there anything I can do to help, Ellie? Shall
I come to the house?'

'No, there's no need for you to do that, Noah.
I expect they'll get tired of waiting and go home

before too long. And I think I'll switch off the landline phone.'

They spoke for a little while longer, and then Noah rang off. Ellie pulled the plug on the phone connection and began to pace the room. She'd tried to sound confident that they would go away, but she wasn't.

She'd had to draw the curtains to stop journalists peering in at her and taking photos through the windows, and she'd had to switch on the lights even though there was daylight outside. She was a prisoner in her own home.

Occasionally, she peeped out through the curtains in the hope that the crowd of photographers and journalists might have gone away but, no, they were still there. She clenched her fists in frustration. What was she going to do?

Then there was a loud rapping at the front door and she froze. She wasn't going to answer it but the knocking went on and a man called out, 'Miss Saunders? I have a letter for you. It's important. Will you please read it now?'

She walked across the hallway and stared at

the white envelope lying on the mat. What now? Was this some new ploy they'd dreamed up? Almost in anger, she snatched up the envelope and ripped it open.

Ellie, I guess things are pretty bad for you right now, so I've asked Charles to come and fetch you. Go with him and he'll bring you to the manor house. You might want to bring an overnight bag with clothes for a couple of days. James.

Relief surged through her. James was there for her, he was thinking about her and offering to help free her from the mob outside. She felt an overwhelming rush of gratitude, and joy, too, that he would come to her rescue, despite what had gone on between them the last time they'd been together. She'd believed she was alone in this, but he'd been thinking of her all the time.

She opened the door a crack. 'Are you Charles?' she asked the young man who was standing there, and when he nodded she beckoned him inside, shutting and locking the door again quickly as the men and women from the tabloids rushed forward in a frenzy of excitement.

'I'm a friend of James,' he explained as they went to the kitchen. He was tall, with a strong physique, and looked capable of handling himself in a difficult situation. Was that why James had chosen him? 'He didn't come himself in case they recognised him. He thought they might follow you to the manor house.'

'That makes sense.' She waved a hand towards the coffee percolator. 'Help yourself to a drink while I go and pack a few things. It's all set up and should be hot.'

'Thank you.'

She was shaking as she bundled a change of clothes into a holdall. How were they going to get through the baying pack outside? After all, Charles was only one man against the crowd.

She pushed her cosmetic case into a corner of the bag and zipped it closed. Then she hurried downstairs and went to find Charles once more.

'I can't think how we're going to get away from here,' she said. 'Even if we're quick, they'll surround us.'

He nodded. 'We thought of that. I parked round the back and walked to the front of the house so they didn't see me drive up. They'll probably assume my car is one of those parked on the road out front. If we go out of here the back way we might be able to fool them. Your car's out front, so they won't be expecting you to leave any other way.'

'Okay. That seems like a good plan.'

A few minutes later they slipped out through the kitchen door and hurried to Charles's car, a long, black saloon with tinted windows.

'So far, so good,' Charles said, as he started up the engine. Then he smoothly drove across the courtyard and out through the stone archway onto the road, where he picked up speed.

'They must have heard us,' Ellie said, looking through the rear-view mirror. 'They're running towards the road.'

Charles smiled. 'Don't worry. They'll never catch up with us now.'

About twenty minutes later they arrived at the manor house and as James came out to greet her, Charles said goodbye. 'You take care.'

'Thank you—thanks for everything,' she called after him, and he acknowledged her with a wave and a smile.

'Hi.' James took hold of her bag and she noticed he, too, was carrying a holdall, the long strap slung over his shoulder. He reached for her, taking her hand in his firm grasp as he led her towards his streamlined silver coupé.

'Hi.' She'd never been so glad to see him. He was long and lean and tautly muscled, every bit her saviour, and she felt safe for the first time in hours. 'Thank you for this,' she said, looking at him with heartfelt gratitude. 'I felt so trapped and frightened, and then all of a sudden you were there for me, giving me a way out.' She would be forever in debt to him for this.

'I knew you must be worried sick. I'm sorry you

had to go through all that.' He unlocked the boot of his car and began to stow their bags inside.

She frowned. 'Where are we going?'

'Where no one will find us,' he said. 'Relax. We're going on a boat trip.'

He held open the passenger-side door, and she slid into the seat. 'A boat trip?' she echoed. 'But what about work in the morning? We have to be at the hospital.'

'Not any more,' he said, starting up the car. 'I've arranged for us to take a couple of days off and brought in locums to take our places.'

Her mouth dropped open. 'Why would you do that?'

He gave her a sideways glance. 'I figured the press will lose interest after a couple of days if they can't find you, and then they'll move on to some other news story.'

She stared at him, wide-eyed. 'This is all so hard to take in. How did you know I was in trouble?'

'I saw the papers this morning. I tried ring-ing you, but you had your phone switched off and the landline was constantly engaged, so I guessed you were having problems. Then I rang Noah and he told me what was going on, so I thought the best thing would be to come and get you, except I didn't want the press to recognise me and put two and two together, so that's where Charles came in.'

'I really appreciate you doing this for me.' She looked at him earnestly and he gave her a brief smile as he turned the car onto the main road. 'I felt so alone and then you sent me that note and it was as if a great weight had been lifted from me.'

'I guessed you needed some help.'

'Thanks again, anyway.' She looked out of the window at the passing landscape, seeing the rolling hills gradually give way to lowland meadows and serene countryside where a river meandered lazily through a gentle valley.

'Where are we headed? What kind of boat trip did you have in mind? I remember you saying once that you have a boat. What kind is it? Is it a yacht?' She looked at him doubtfully. She wasn't sure she wanted to go sailing on a wide, choppy sea.

'Nothing as grand as that. Ever since I was a child I've enjoyed cruising the inland waterways, so a couple of years ago I decided to buy a canal boat. Now, whenever I get the chance, I like to spend leisurely weekends on the water. That's where we're going.'

'It sounds great.' She smiled. 'It'll be a new experience for me.'

'Then I hope you like it. The boat's fitted out with most things we might need for a comfortable journey.'

Ellie thought about his leisurely weekends. Had Sophie spent time with him on the boat? Her stomach lurched and she quickly pushed the unwanted image from her mind. James was doing this for her and she should be grateful for that. It wouldn't help to dwell on the woman who was unwittingly driving a wedge between them.

They finally arrived at their destination and

James parked the car at the marina, where a dozen or so colourful boats were moored.

'Here we are. This one's mine, the *Louise Jane.*'

Ellie made a quick guess. 'Is she named after your mother?'

He nodded. 'That's right. I wanted something special to keep her memory alive.'

Unexpectedly, Ellie's eyes dampened. It was a wonderful gesture, a loving tribute from a son who had lost his mother at a young age. It was something his mother would have truly appreciated.

The boat was long, and a pleasing dark green, with distinctive artwork painted across its length. There were pictures of flowers in bright reds and yellows, and other canal art showing watering cans and colourful tubs.

'Let's go on board,' James said, 'and I'll show you around.'

He held her hand, supporting her as she stepped onto the deck, and then he closed the rail and led the way down wooden steps into the galley. Immediately, she missed his warm hand clasping hers. 'I had her fitted out with a top-of-the-range cooker and fridge and as many cupboards as possible.'

'This is really impressive, James.' All the equipment was modern, and the stainless-steel surfaces gleamed softly. The floor was covered in warm-looking, solid oak timbers.

He acknowledged her praise with a faint inclination of his head. 'I stocked the fridge and the cupboards recently and I've brought a few essentials with me, so we should manage well enough.'

She pulled in a deep breath. It was only just beginning to dawn on her that she and James would be alone on this boat for the next couple of days. It wasn't something she might ever have imagined, especially since they had left each other in strained circumstances just a short time ago. Now, though, her treacherous body responded by being both excited and unnerved at the same time.

'Come through to the main cabin,' he said,

ushering her into what looked like a cosy sitting room.

There were plush, upholstered bench seats on opposite sides, decorated with bright cushions, and in one corner there was an oak table large enough to accommodate four people.

'The seats lift up, so there's more storage space underneath,' he explained, and she looked around admiringly.

'Do you sleep in here?' she asked, imagining sleeping bags laid out along the length of the seats. And that gave rise to a worrying question in her mind. Where would they both sleep tonight? How would she cope, being so near to him?

'No. There are separate sleeping berths—partitioned off to allow some privacy. I'll show you, and you can choose which one you want.' He glanced at her, his mouth making a devilish twist. 'Unless, of course, you'd like to share with me? It can get chilly out on the water at night, and I'd be more than happy to keep you warm.'

Heat washed through her from head to toe at

his suggestion. 'I'm sure you would,' she murmured, 'but somehow I don't think that would be a good idea.'

'A pity, that,' he said, giving her a rueful glance. 'I thought it was an excellent one. But if you should change your mind...'

'I'm sorry, but I won't.' It grieved her to say it, but she'd made up her mind not to get involved with him. Her reputation was in tatters, and getting close to him would only lead to heartache in the end because they were worlds apart. He came from a family of meticulously respectable ancestors, and she simply wouldn't fit in. Especially now, since her face had been splashed over all the papers.

And yet he'd taken her rejection of him with good humour, as always. It was so heart-warming to have him look after her this way. He'd asked nothing of her. He was a truly wonderful man, like none she'd ever known. Who else would have taken care of her like this, without expecting something in return?

He took her through to the sleeping quarters,

each room furnished with a double bed and overhead cupboard space, and lastly he showed her what he called 'the head', which was where the bathroom facilities were housed. Again, these were the best quality with pearl-white porcelain fittings.

'I'll start up the motor and get us under way,' he said, as they walked back towards the galley. 'Then when we're away further along the canal we'll stop for a bite to eat. I'd suggest we stop at a pub, but with your picture being splashed over the papers, people who've seen you on TV might be tempted to hassle you. What do you think?'

'I think you're probably right,' she said in a dejected tone. 'I feel as though my life's been turned upside down. I just don't know why any of this is happening or who could have done it. Who would want to ruin my life, and my TV career?'

He put his arms around her and gave her a quick hug. 'I can't imagine anyone who would want to do something like this. Everyone I know likes you. You're sweet, kind and thoughtful, and you certainly don't deserve to be pilloried this way. Neither does Lewis. It's abominable how they've pointed the finger at him.'

He released her all too soon, and Ellie struggled to bring her chaotic senses under control. She followed him up on deck.

James untied the mooring rope and started up the motor, steering them slowly along the watercourse. He looked perfectly at ease at the wheel, completely in command. He was wearing khaki chinos and a dark T-shirt that emphasised his powerful biceps, and Ellie had a strange compulsion to run her hands over his strong arms and feel his body tauten next to hers.

With a supreme effort of will she resisted the urge. Instead, she said quietly, 'I rang Lewis's wife and told her there's no truth in the stories. She seemed thoroughly shocked by what's happening and Lewis is doing his utmost to put her mind at rest.'

'They've been struggling lately,' James remarked. 'I don't know exactly what the problem is, but Lewis admits they've been arguing far more than usual. They've been married for about five years, and up till now things have gone well for them, or so it seemed.'

'And you blame me for getting in the way?'

He gave her a sideways look. 'He may not have said anything, but Lewis is very susceptible to your charms. I think he's flattered because you're a good listener, you have a sympathetic ear, and it's easy to see how his head might have been turned.'

'But that's all in your imagination. Surely you know that? There has never been anything going on between Lewis and me. Why would you think otherwise?'

'Because Lewis is vulnerable, and it would be very easy for him to be open to temptation. It would ruin him if he succumbed, because he really does love his wife. Far better, then, for you to try to steer clear of him.'

'Don't you think Lewis and I can sort things out between us?'

'Unfortunately, no. But I certainly feel more at ease knowing you're on this boat with me, rather than getting together with Lewis to offer each other sympathy and understanding. Lewis is already in a fragile state emotionally. Having you close at hand could make any man go weak at the knees.'

She frowned, uneasy at what he was saying. 'Is that why you brought me here?'

'I brought you here to make sure you were safe and out of reach of the press. Keeping you out of reach of Lewis is an added bonus.'

She bit back a sharp comment. After all, she could hardly take him to task for that when he had saved her from being trapped in her own home. She didn't want to be at odds with him, but inside she fretted at his lack of faith in her. What made him doubt her? Was it some subconscious conviction that women weren't to be relied on? That they would somehow manage to cause hurt? A sad relic of his mother leaving him, perhaps, albeit that she'd done it unwillingly?

Surely she was the one who was most likely to be feeling insecure in that way? Her mother had deserted her—hadn't that led to the wild teen-age years that were her undoing now?

She sighed. 'Shall I go below and put the kettle on? I could prepare some food if you like. I don't know about you, but I haven't eaten today. I lost my appetite when I saw the papers, and the rest is history.'

'That's a good idea, if you don't mind doing that. There are cooked meats in the fridge and some bread. Help yourself to whatever you want. I expect sandwiches will be the easiest. I'll come and give you a hand as soon as I find a place to moor the boat.'

'Okay.'

She went to the galley and looked inside the fridge and the cupboards. As he'd said, they were well stocked. There was rice, a variety of meats, peppers and vegetables, some mushrooms and onions. Pushing back the sleeves of her blouse, she washed her hands and set about making a meal. She could do better than sandwiches.

'Hey, something smells good,' James said,

coming down the steps to the galley some time later. 'What's cooking?'

'Chicken risotto. It seemed like the easiest thing to do. And I've made a fruit salad for dessert. All of a sudden I'm starving.'

He grinned. 'Me, too. I can't wait to try it. Shall we eat up on deck? We may as well make the most of this lovely weather while it lasts. Before we know it, we'll be into October and it'll be coats and scarves at the ready, unless we're lucky.'

'Yes, okay. Shall I make us a drink to take up there?'

'I'll open a bottle of wine. You serve up and I'll see to the drinks and carry everything up top.'

'All right.'

They sat on bench seats by the boat rail and tucked into the meal while watching ducks dip in and out of the reeds at the water's edge. The canal had opened out here and wildlife flourished. Birds flew down to catch insects that hovered over the thistles and sedge on the banks, and a somnolent, leisurely atmosphere pervaded overall. Ellie leaned back and relaxed, watching nature at its best.

'This is delicious,' James said, savouring the different flavours of the risotto. 'When you said you liked cooking, I didn't know you could throw a few ingredients together and make something like this. It's mouthwatering.'

'I'm glad you think so.'

He poured wine, chilled from the fridge, and they clinked glasses together in a toast. 'Good health and good times,' James said.

Ellie echoed the toast. 'Yes, let's hope for those,' she said, sipping the wine and feeling its soothing coolness slide down her throat. 'I wonder what sort of times lie ahead. You have your future mapped out for you, I expect, as it has been through the generations. And at least I have my hospital career to rely on.'

He was preoccupied for a moment, thinking about that, and then he said quietly, 'Have you heard anything from your TV producer?'

She shook her head. 'No. But all this is bound

to affect my future there. He was planning to go ahead with a new series, but I dare say this will have put a spoke in that idea. He won't want a disreputable doctor presenting the programmes.'

'Surely most people will realise that you were still a teenager back then? If they knew something of your background they would understand why you behaved as you did.' He watched the variety of expressions flit across her face. 'Perhaps it's time to bring all of that out into the open—talk about how you felt lost and alone, and this was your way of expressing all your teenage angst. You rebelled against the system and against the adults who had let you down. Why would people hold that against you?'

'I don't know. But someone obviously wanted it shouted to all and sundry. They must have known it would ruin my career in television.' She frowned and sipped more wine, then looked at him pensively. 'You're being very understanding about all this. I would have thought that with your background and everything, with your father being a stickler for the right way of going about things, you might disapprove of me.'

'I'm not my father.'

'No.' But she knew there would never be any place for her in his life. Throughout their long history, his family had been proud, deeply traditional, and conservative in outlook. They would never countenance accepting a notorious individual into their midst.

That thought had dropped into her mind without any warning. When had it happened that she'd started to yearn for more than a casual relationship, for something meaningful and secure?

James topped up her wineglass and ate the last of his risotto. 'Anyway, I feel that we're partly to blame for what happened to you and your family and I can understand why Noah felt so strongly.'

'He said he regrets what he did. I don't think he realised until now how devastating it can be to come across things that have been written about you and spread out in the papers for all to see.'

'I know. He apologised to me this morning, and asked me to pass on his regrets to my father. He said he's going to write to him.'

'Will it make a difference to your father?'

'Possibly. He certainly feels some responsibility for your father's troubles since he discovered that he had been ill.'

They started on their desserts and waved to a passing canal-boat crew, though Ellie turned her head a little and let her hair draw a curtain over her features to stop her from being recognised.

'Why am I doing this?' she said in exasperation when the boat had travelled into the distance. 'I can't hide for ever, can I? Sooner or later I'm going to have to face up to things, and the public.'

'There's time enough to work out how to do that,' James said. 'Just take it easy for now. You've been through a traumatic time today, and you need to come to terms with it in your own mind before you take on the world again. I'm sure we'll think of something.'

She smiled, letting her gaze wander over his

face and explore his perfect features. She wasn't alone. He was by her side, and he would help her to get through this. It made her stronger, simply knowing that.

The following day they travelled further along the canal, negotiating a series of locks along the way. Each time James jumped onto the towpath and turned the key to open the sluice, while Ellie helped pull the lock gates into position to allow them through to continue their journey.

'I can see why people take to this way of life,' she said that evening as they ate supper on the deck in the moonlight. 'There's no hurrying, no rush to do anything. You have to take your time, and after a while, without realising it's happened, you find the tranquillity has seeped into your bones.'

'It's certainly a good antidote to working in A and E,' James said with a smile. 'I'm glad you've taken to it. You definitely seem more relaxed now, more at ease with everything.'

'It's been perfect. I hadn't realised how much I needed to get away—to get right away—from everything and everyone. I feel so much better now, ready to face up to things.'

'That's what I was hoping for.' James took a long swallow of his chilled lager and offered to top up her wineglass with what was left in the bottle cooling on ice.

'Thanks.' She was in a dreamy, hazy state of bliss, at peace with herself for the first time in ages. 'And thank you for all this, James. It's been a great experience.' It had been wonderful just to be with him and she wanted this time to go on and on and never end.

She drained her glass and reluctantly got to her feet. 'It's late,' she said. 'I should go to bed. I'm wiped out—in a good way.' She didn't want to leave him but she was afraid to start something that might get out of hand. She cared deeply for him, was falling in love with him, but she was desperately afraid of being hurt.

'Goodnight, Ellie.'

She couldn't be sure, in the shadows cast by the silver light of the moon, but it seemed there was a yearning, regretful glimmer in the depths of his smoke-dark eyes.

She felt the same aching need for him as she lay restlessly on her bed, all too conscious of him in the next berth. The air was warm, and heavy with an electric tension, a vibrant, throbbing sense of unfulfilled, heady desire.

In the morning she woke up after hearing a knock on the door and some words that she couldn't make out through the drowsy mist of sleep. She stretched lazily, feeling slightly disorientated and with her head filled with remnants of dreams. They had been good dreams that in her semi-conscious state made her feel upbeat, as though the world was her oyster.

Some time later she became aware of the appetising smell of frying bacon, and James was knocking on the partition door once again, saying, 'Wake up, sleepyhead. Your breakfast is ready. You need to get yourself in here now.'

She scrambled out of bed and hurried to splash water on her face and wake herself up. Then she threw on a short silk robe that she'd had the presence of mind to bundle into her holdall, and went in search of that wonderful smell.

'Ah, there you are.' James must have caught sight of her out of the corner of his eye as he lifted a frying pan from the hob. 'I was thinking I'd have to come and haul you out of bed.'

Then he looked at her properly and suddenly became still, an arrested expression in his eyes and in the silent whistle that hovered on his lips. He put down the pan he was holding. 'On second thoughts, it's just as well I didn't come to get you.' His gaze shimmered over her, lingering on the silk that clung to her curves, before drifting down along her bare legs to her carefully painted toenails. 'That way, we'd never have got around to breakfast.'

She laughed, and looked at the preparations he'd made. The table was set with cutlery, a rack of toast and a covered teapot alongside two cups. 'Is there anything I can do to help?'

'Uh, yeah, maybe you could cover yourself with a sack and then I might be able to concentrate better.'

She chuckled, leaning negligently against the doorjamb. He looked pretty good himself, tall and flat stomached, strong and capable, a feast for her senses first thing in the morning. 'Is something disturbing you?' she enquired teasingly.

'Oh, yes, I'd say so. A slinky, sensual, gorgeous creature with curves in all the right places and a mane of hair that is sinfully sexy.' He shook his head as though freeing himself of a troublesome image and began to absently dish out golden-centred fried eggs, sliding them onto plates that had been warmed in the oven.

Then he gave up the fight with his willpower and left everything where it was, and came over to her. 'What the heck. I'm just a man and you're a temptress beyond imagining. What am I to do, Ellie?'

'Hmm…let's see. You could kiss me,' she said huskily. 'Do you think that would solve your problem?'

'I think it might go a long way.' He didn't need a second bidding. He took her into his arms and his whole body seemed to quiver with pent-up need, so much so that for a fleeting second or two she wondered if she should have thought this through. She could be taking on a whole lot more than she could handle.

Then his mouth crushed hers in a kiss that heated her blood and turned her whole body to flame, while his hands drew her up against his firm body and pressured her soft curves until it felt as though they had meshed together as one.

'I need you, Ellie,' he said raggedly. 'I want you so much.'

His hands sought out the smooth arc of her hips and swept upwards, seeking out the soft swell of her breasts. He cupped her gently, caressing her with exquisite expertise, bringing a low moan of contentment to her lips. His thumbs made a light, circling motion, tantalising her with sweet forays into the pleasure zone,and rousing her until she trembled with desire.

She ran her hands over him, memorising every flat plane and velvet-covered muscle, wanting to lay her cheek against him and feel the thunderous beat of his heart.

He kissed her again, a glorious, passionate, seeking kiss, and she responded wholeheartedly, her lips parting beneath his so that she could savour his sweet, warm possession.

Then, like the dash of a sudden, cold shower, a hooter sounded, long and loud, and they broke apart, looking about them in time to see another canal boat gliding past.

Ellie was breathing deeply, trying to get over the shock of the sudden separation, and James simply stared into space for a moment, caught in a strange kind of limbo.

He braced himself and exhaled slowly. 'Ellie...'

'Perhaps it's just as well we were disturbed,' she said. The dreamy haze was rapidly clearing from her mind and she was coming to see that getting close to him had been a big mistake. 'I should never have started that. It was wrong of me. Can we put it down to some sort of temporary lack of judgement?'

'Was it?'

'I think it must have been.'

Imagining that she could be with him was just a dream, beautiful while it had lasted, but now she had to try and get back to reality. She didn't want a brief fling with him. She wanted the one thing he couldn't give her. Commitment.

CHAPTER EIGHT

'HAVE YOU THOUGHT any more about talking to the press and giving your side of the story?' James asked as they drove home late that afternoon. 'You could point out where they had their facts wrong, and explain about the things that happened in your childhood to make you get into trouble.'

'I can't do that,' she said. 'It means I'd have to talk about my parents—about my mother leaving us. I won't do it. I won't say bad things about my family to the world at large. They'll either have to take me as I am and trust in me to be the kind of person they want to believe in, or follow what the papers say about me. There will always be people who think the worst.'

Wasn't that what happened whenever James saw her with Lewis? His problem was that he had to learn to trust, and until that happened, their relationship was doomed.

'Anyway, I'd far sooner find out who started these tales and ask why they did it.' Her brows drew together. 'Do you think Mel could have been behind them? I can't think of anyone else who might bear a grudge against me.'

He gave it some thought. 'It's possible, I suppose. She was certainly angry and upset, and she wasn't satisfied with the result of our initial meeting. But she'd most likely deny it if you asked her and the papers won't reveal their sources.'

'That's true.' She sighed, frustrated by the lack of any possible action. It was upsetting to think that a woman she had known so well throughout her teenage years could have done something so vindictive.

In a while they pulled up outside the manor house and James parked the car on the drive.

'I'll take you home in a while,' he said, 'but I'm anxious to see if my father's all right. That last phone call from him earlier this afternoon made me suspect something was wrong. He didn't sound like his usual self.'

'You're bound to be worried about him.' Ellie went with him into the house, marvelling once more at its understated grandeur. Solid oak beams pointed to its historic origins and the spaciousness of the layout added to the feeling of stateliness and old money.

Lord Birchenall was in the drawing room, talking on the phone, and it was fairly clear that he was annoyed about something.

'There's no question about me harassing you over the land,' he said sharply. 'It was clearly written into the agreement I made with your stepfather a long time ago. The land was to revert to me after a period of ten years. All I'm doing is asking you to honour that agreement.'

He cut the call a few minutes later, breathing heavily. Ellie could hear the wheezing in his chest, and noticed that his cheeks were drained of colour.

'You promised you would leave me to deal with that,' James gently admonished his father.

'There's no need for you to be getting yourself in a state about it. We'll let the lawyers deal with the matter.'

'You have enough to do, running the estate,' Lord Birchenall protested.

'That doesn't matter. You shouldn't be getting hot and bothered about these things when I can take the worry from you.'

Ellie could see that it was all too much for James's father. He looked feverish and his breathing was getting faster and more laboured. He put a hand to his chest and began to cough, all signs that his lungs were drowning in fluid as a result of his heart problems.

She caught James's glance. 'I'll go and get my medical bag,' he said, suddenly on alert. 'His GTN spray is in the bureau drawer.'

She went to get the spray and gave it to his father, who had sunk down into a chair. He used the medication, which was supposed to help relieve the pain, and then she took his pulse. It was erratic, and that was worrying.

'James won't be able to run this place as well

as do his job at the hospital,' Lord Birchenall said, his voice rasping. 'We need to sort things out...get some system in place...'

Ellie loosened his collar and said softly, 'I'm sure James will manage very well. Try to stay calm. We're here to look after you. You should rest.'

'He needs to marry and settle down. Sophie's ideal for him, they're well suited, and she'll make him a good wife. He needs to ensure his future here.'

Ellie's heart contracted at his words. All this talk of James and Sophie played on her worst fears. Was his future all mapped out? Had the time he'd spent with her this weekend been a simple dalliance? But she didn't have time to dwell on any of that because James's father was gasping now, and she was desperate to calm him down.

Lord Birchenall leaned forward, clutching his chest. The spray obviously hadn't helped him.

'You don't need to worry about any of that right now,' she said. 'Just try to take things easy.' They needed to get him on oxygen and give him some medication to reduce the amount of fluid on his lungs. 'We'll give you something for the pain. It won't be long now.'

But before they could do any of that, before James had returned with his medical kit, Lord Birchenall suddenly slumped and slid down in his chair, gradually losing consciousness.

Ellie couldn't find a pulse this time, and urgently called out to James for help. Then, after using her mobile to call for an ambulance, she used all her strength to carefully tug his father down on to the floor so that she could give him CPR.

When James hurried into the room, she was on her knees by his father's side, doing chest compressions to try to force the blood around his body. 'His heart stopped,' she said. 'Do you have a defibrillator?'

'Yes, right here.' His voice was taut with concern because he knew as well as she did that once the heart had stopped pumping, blood couldn't get around the body, and if that happened, the patient would die within a very short time.

James hurriedly set up the defibrillator, attaching the pads to his father's chest. All the time Ellie went on with the compressions.

'It's charged. Stay clear.'

She stopped the CPR and moved back a little while the machine delivered a shock to the heart. To their dismay, nothing changed, and as the unit detected that it had been unsuccessful it began to charge again. A second shock, more powerful than the first, followed.

This time a cardiac rhythm showed up on the monitor and James breathed a sigh of relief. He gave his father oxygen through a mask, while Ellie injected their patient with a painkiller and a diuretic that would help to reduce the fluid in his lungs.

'The ambulance should be here any minute now,' she told Lord Birchenall, and he nodded, dazed and uncertain about what had happened to him but beginning to recover a little.

The ambulance arrived and the paramedics came to tend to him. 'Are you coming with your father to the hospital?' one of them asked James.

'Yes. I'll throw a few things into a bag for him. They'll want to keep him in.'

'Okay. You might want to go and do that while we get him on a stretcher and transfer him to the vehicle.'

'I will.' James turned to Ellie and lightly squeezed her arm. 'Thank you for what you did. You saved his life.'

'We did it together,' she said, going with him to the stairs.

'I'm sorry you walked into all this,' he murmured, 'and I wish I didn't have to leave you this way. It wasn't the way I wanted our two days together to end.'

'It's okay.' Her mind was filled with doubts now about that time. She wanted him more than ever, but she couldn't see any way that would happen. He wasn't ready for any lasting relationship, unless he was planning to be with Sophie, as his father had suggested. 'I just hope your father's going to be all right.'

He sighed. 'So do I. Look, I hate to let you down—I'll call for a taxi to take you home.'

'No, I'll see to that. You need to concentrate on your father,' she told him. 'Go and pack some essentials. The paramedics will be ready to go any minute.'

He went upstairs and Ellie dialled the number for a taxi. She was sad for James that this had happened. He loved his father and his mind must be in turmoil.

When he came back downstairs she quickly searched his face. Her heart went out to him and she laid a comforting hand on his arm, knowing how anxious he was. He reacted warmly, giving her a quick a hug.

'Thanks again for all your help, Ellie,' he said as they walked back to the drawing room. 'It's a worry. These episodes are becoming more and more frequent.'

'I know, but let's be thankful we were both here with him.'

His hands lightly circled her arms. 'You're a treasure…in lots of ways.' He gave a half-smile. 'These last couple of days have been extra-special.'

'Yes, they were.' Her expression sobered as she saw the taxi draw up outside and the driver hooted his horn. 'I had a lovely time. Thank you for helping me to get away from everything.'

'Any time you need me, I'll be there.' He walked with her to the door and hesitated, obviously reluctant to see her go, but he said quietly, 'I'll come and see you tomorrow after work, just to make sure everything's all right.'

'Okay.'

She climbed into the taxi and waved goodbye as the vehicle moved away swiftly. She tried not to think about what Lord Birchenall had said, but his words echoed inside her head. He wanted his son to marry the daughter of one of his dearest friends. Was that what James wanted, too?

Her house was mercifully free of journalists lying in wait for her when she arrived home, and she went inside feeling relieved about that and prepared to get back into her normal routine.

She sat down at the kitchen table. When she'd switched on her mobile phone for the first time in two days, a number of text messages had started to come in. One was from her father, offering support, and she answered that, pleased that he had contacted her. Another was from her TV producer, asking her to get in touch.

I can drop by your place on Thursday evening, he wrote. *I'll be in the area then. Will you let me know if that's okay?*

Her stomach knotted briefly, but she knew this was something she would have to face up to eventually. Bracing herself, she answered him, setting up the meeting for Thursday.

Still worried by what had happened with the press, Ellie double-checked that she had locked all her doors and windows before she went to bed. If someone disliked her enough to set the newshounds on her, what else might they do?

But nothing happened during the night, and she woke up and got ready for work as usual in the morning. She was on edge the whole time. What kind of reception would she get at the hospital?

'Ellie, I feel really bad about what happened,' Lewis said later that morning when he came and found her in Accident and Emergency. 'How have you been?'

'I've been all right.' She studied his worried expression. 'What about you and Jessica? It must have been very distressing for you.'

He nodded, taking her to one side where they could talk more privately. Even so, she was aware of James watching them from a distance as he came out of the resuscitation room. His gaze was dark and contemplative, and she wished she knew what he was thinking. He'd been tied up with an emergency all morning and she hadn't had a chance to speak to him yet.

'I suppose the only good thing is that it made Jessica and I talk about things more than we have been doing of late,' Lewis said. 'We've not been getting on all that well these last few months, and I suppose this brought things to a head. We haven't resolved our problems yet, but at least we're going some way towards it.'

'I hope you manage to work things out.'

'So do I. Thanks.'

He went back to his own unit after a few minutes, and Ellie started to read through the notes on her next patient, frowning a little as she saw the test results.

James came over to her. 'Are you getting on all right?' he asked. 'Are people treating you well?'

She nodded and gave him a quick smile. 'They've been marvellous, really. Those who saw the papers are angry that they printed the stories. They say it was all sensationalism. But, of course, that's what seems to sell papers these days.'

'I'm glad you're all right. If you do have any problems, let me know.'

'I will, but I think I can handle things now. I feel much stronger mentally.' She had to be strong to face up to losing her TV career. It was something she'd built up over the years and she felt she was reaching out to a lot of people through the medium of television. It would be a wrench to have to let it go.

She sent him a pensive glance, conscious that he had worries of his own. 'How is your father? Is he holding up?'

He hesitated. 'He seems to be making a recovery of sorts. It's difficult to predict exactly how he'll do because, as you know, his heart was already failing, and this latest attack has only made things worse. They'll be keeping him in the cardiac wing for a few days at least.'

'I suppose that was to be expected. Does he need anything? Can I help in any way, with books or magazines, or anything? Noah has a collection of audio tapes about stately homes that might interest him.'

'I'm sure he'd welcome those, if Noah doesn't mind him borrowing them.'

'It would be Noah's way of trying to put things right, perhaps. At some point we have to let go of the past and move on.'

'Thanks. It's a great idea and it will help to take his mind off things. Sophie's getting together some books for him, but I'm not sure he's up to concentrating on the printed word just yet.'

He glanced at her. 'You know, he's really grateful to you for stepping in and keeping his heart going for those vital minutes. He's been asking about you, and he asked me to thank you for what you did.'

'I appreciate that.' She was trying not to read anything into his casual mention of Sophie, but an image of the two of them getting together persisted. 'It's good that he came through it all right. It was a nasty experience for him.'

James smiled at her, and then straightened his shoulders, as though trying to shrug off a heavy burden. He glanced down at the file in her hands. 'Do you have any worries with any of your patients? You looked as though you were troubled when you were looking through those notes.'

She shook her head. 'Not really, except it looks as though this lady's symptoms are similar to my father's. To be honest, it brought back memories I'd rather forget.'

He frowned and she explained, 'It was a bad time for us as a family when he started to become ill, and I didn't really understand what was happening. We thought he had lost interest in his work. Now, though, when I see these symptoms in other people, I realise what my father was going through.'

She turned the pages of the patient's file. 'This lady, for instance. She often feels faint and can't summon up any energy. She's confused sometimes, and any slight infection or viral illness makes her feel much worse. She came here today by ambulance in a state of collapse, so obviously things are pretty bad for her. Her heart rate is very high, she's breathing rapidly, and she has a fever and joint pain.'

'You think she has Addison's disease?'

'I do. I've run some tests, and I'm going to give her an intravenous injection of hydrocortisone. She'll need an infusion of saline with dextrose, too. That should help to calm things down for the moment.'

He went with her towards the treatment room. 'Do you know why your father carried on without telling anyone he was ill?'

She shook her head. 'I think he believed he was just a bit under the weather and tried to muddle through. He didn't want to admit to any kind of weakness. It was only after he lost his job and the marriage broke down that the stress became too much for him. He went to the doctor and was treated for various complaints over time—none of them the correct diagnosis. Then, finally, his body couldn't cope with the demand on his adrenal cortex any longer. That's when he ended up in hospital and they found the real cause of his illness.'

'He must have been in a bad way...mentally and physically.'

'Yes, he was. But thankfully things are under control now, and he seems to be keeping fairly healthy. He just has to be careful if he gets an infection—then he has to take corticosteroids and perhaps antibiotics.'

He draped an arm around her shoulders. 'All I can say is that I'm sorry you had to go through that. If we'd known, we could have done something to help.'

'Do you think your father would have kept him on? I have the feeling he wants things to run smoothly, and he'll see it happen at any cost.'

'That might have been true at one time, but I think he might have mellowed a bit since then.'

'Perhaps.'

She went into the treatment room to see her patient, and James said softly, 'I'll come and see you this evening after work, as I promised. Just in case the press decide to come back. I may be a little late because I'll look in on my father first.'

'Um, you might want to change your mind about that—my producer is coming to see me. I think I'm about to get the sack.' She would have liked him to be with her this evening—just having him there would give her the confidence to face anything, but he would most likely stay away if he knew she wasn't going to be alone.

He pulled a face. 'The tide will turn,' he said. 'Things can only get better.'

She thought about that when she was at home, getting ready for Ben's visit. She dressed in a pretty pintucked shirt and a pencil-line skirt, on the premise that if she started out looking her best, she would feel brighter about the way things might turn out.

'I guessed you must be feeling low after what's been going on,' Ben said when she showed him into the sitting room a bit later on. 'We've had a lot of emails and calls at the studio.'

'You have? I'm sorry about that.'

He smiled. 'Don't be. You have a lot of really steadfast fans out there—a lot of them are male, it has to be said, but there were a good many letters from female viewers, too. They think it was wrong for them to have printed articles about events that happened when you were still in your teens.'

'That's good to know.' She brightened a little and then said, 'But how do we go on from here? Does it mean an end to the next series you were planning?'

'I'm not sure,' he said. 'We'd need to find a way of ensuring that the viewers are all on your side, one hundred per cent. It means they'd need to know what went on back then to cause you to go off the rails. Perhaps if you start by telling me what happened?'

She told him and gave him a few minutes to

let him absorb what she'd said. She made coffee and brought it into the sitting room on a tray.

'How are we going to let people know?' he
mused. 'Do we put out a statement to the press,
or maybe deal with it in a separate programme?'

'I can't tell them about my past and what happened to my family. It would be too much like
a betrayal.'

'Even though, in a way, *you* were betrayed?
After all, you lost your home and your mother
left you and your brother. That must have been
a terrible blow when you were so young, and it
had to have played a big part in sending you off
track.'

'Maybe.' She thought about it, trying to make
sense of her chaotic emotions. 'It was really hard
for us to come to terms with what was happening at the time, but when I look back on it now
I realise that both of my parents were suffering,
too. After all, my mother was ill with depression and simply couldn't cope with the situation
and the responsibilities of a family. Everything

must have overwhelmed her and my father. But, of course, I didn't see that then.

'I was bitter and resentful and reacted by doing exactly as I pleased, regardless of the consequences. No matter what's happened now, I can't dismiss my own failings by putting the blame on my parents and throwing it all back in their faces.'

She tried to think of some way she could put things right. 'I suppose I could apologise for my behaviour and explain that it all happened when I was young and immature. Perhaps say that I've managed to turn my life around.'

'Unfortunately, I don't think that will be enough,' he said with a shake of his head. 'It seems we have a problem.'

They talked for a while longer, trying to think of ways around the situation, and eventually he stood up to go, saying, 'I'll give it some more thought and see if I can come up with something. Maybe we could do a series of programmes about children's problems, psychological worries, teenage angst and so on.'

That sounded encouraging, unless, of course, he decided to choose another presenter to do these programmes. That would be a bitter blow after she'd worked so hard to establish a career for herself.

She'd had to drag herself out of that downward spiral of recklessness that had threatened to destroy her, and instead put her energy into doing something worthwhile.

When she had been at her lowest ebb she had realised she was throwing her life away. After yet another all-night party her friend had fallen and injured herself and Ellie had been horrified to see blood pouring from a head wound.

She had hardly been in a fit state to help her. She'd managed to call for an ambulance and had held a towel to her friend's head to try to stem the bleeding, but the whole incident had been a wake-up call.

After her friend had recovered, Ellie had decided she would sort herself out once and for all. That's when she'd made up her mind that she would study medicine.

Now, though, her TV career was in jeopardy, and all she could do was wait and see whether it would fail completely.

It would have cheered her to see James this evening, but there had been no sign of him. Even though she'd suggested he might want to stay away, she was saddened and disappointed by his absence. A part of her had hoped he would want to be with her.

But perhaps he had chosen to be with Sophie instead. After all, Sophie was a regular visitor to the manor house, and she would want to sympathise with him over his father's heart attack. It was only natural that they would be together.

CHAPTER NINE

'WE'RE GOING TO need ice packs and cooling blankets, Olivia. Her temperature's way too high. She'll need paracetamol every four hours to keep it down.'

'I'll see to it.'

'Thanks.' Ellie frowned as she wrote out the prescription form. Her patient, a woman in her late thirties, was very ill. The ECG showed an abnormal cardiac rhythm and she was feverish and sweating profusely. She could scarcely get her breath and was being given oxygen through a mask.

'I'm going to put her on a dextrose drip. Her body's gone into overdrive and is making way too many demands on her system. Her heart's racing, her blood pressure's off the scale—if we don't act quickly, she's heading towards seizures and heart failure.'

Olivia pulled a face. 'Perhaps it's no wonder she's irritable. She told me to stop fussing around her and to leave her alone. She must be feeling awful.'

Ellie nodded. 'I think the irritability is part of the illness. I won't know for sure until the test results come back, but I think we're dealing with a thyroid storm here. Too much thyroid hormone in the bloodstream.'

Ellie set up the drip while Olivia went to fetch the ice packs.

'Jenny,' she said gently, trying to reassure the woman, 'I'm going to give you some medication to calm your heart's activity down a bit and we'll do what we can to make you feel more comfortable while we're waiting for the lab results to come back. In the meantime, I'll make arrangements for you to be admitted to one of the wards.'

'Okay. Whatever.' Jenny was too exhausted to say anything more.

Ellie recognised that her agitation was simply a part of her condition, and she went on trying to explain things. 'When you're more settled, I'll ask a nurse to take you along to Radiology for a chest X-ray so that we can see what's going on.' If the heart had been overworking for any length of time, there was a possibility of heart failure, leading to a build-up of fluid on the lungs.

Ellie made sure that everything possible was being done for the woman, and then she went to check up on her other patients. She glanced around to see if James was working in one of the treatment rooms, but there was no sign of him. In fact, she hadn't seen him all morning and that was puzzling—but perhaps it wasn't altogether unusual if he had a meeting to attend.

Even so, she missed him. She'd looked for him first thing, and when she'd discovered he wasn't here, she'd half expected him to ring her and say something about last night. Instead, there had been silence, and that was odd, especially when he knew she'd been concerned about the meeting with Ben.

There must be a reason why he hadn't come to see her or tried to get in touch.

Those two days she'd spent with him on the boat had been wonderful. They'd made her realise that she wanted to be with him all the time—that he was the only man who could make her truly happy. It had been just a couple of days, but it had been long enough for her to know that she'd fallen in love with him.

And that was a foolhardy thing to have done, wasn't it, because she had no way of knowing if he would eventually lose interest in her. She would be devastated if that happened...and yet he had warned her. He'd said all he wanted was a casual relationship, but the tragedy was she'd discovered that she wanted much more than that.

'I rang up and enquired about the two patients you were asking about,' Olivia said, breaking into her thoughts as she came over to the desk where Ellie was checking the computer for test results.

'You did?' She pulled herself together. 'Thanks,

Olivia. I haven't found a minute to do it myself. What's happening with them?'

'The lady with the heart inflammation is beginning to respond to the antibiotics, and is generally much better. The consultant has removed the drain and is positive about her recovery.'

Ellie smiled, relieved by the news. 'That's brilliant. I was so worried when she came in.' Then she frowned. 'What about Mr Langley, our patient with pancreatitis? Did you manage to get an update on him?'

Olivia nodded. 'He's had surgery to remove the obstruction, and he's being resuscitated with fluids. He's on antibiotic therapy, too, and seems to be doing well.'

'I'm glad about that. Thanks for chasing it up for me.'

'You're welcome.'

Ellie glanced at her watch. 'Time's gone a lot faster than I realised. I'd better go and take my lunch break.'

'You're a bit late with that, aren't you?' Olivia raised a brow. 'I went for mine ages ago.'

'It happens that way sometimes when we're busy. Anyway, I'm going to have a quick bite to eat, and then I'll go over to the cardiac unit.'

'Is that where James's father's being treated?'

'That's right. I have some audio tapes for him.'

She went off and helped herself to a quick snack in the cafeteria and then headed over to the cardiac unit. With any luck, Lord Birchenall would be feeling much brighter by now and would enjoy listening to the tapes.

He was receiving treatment in the private wing of the hospital, and Ellie needed directions to his room, but the nurse on Reception seemed cautious about letting her see him.

'I don't think…uh…I mean…uh…his son is in there. I don't think he should be disturbed.'

Ellie frowned. 'Has he taken a turn for the worse?'

'Um…yes, I'm afraid so. In fact…he died just over an hour ago.' She frowned. 'I'm very sorry.'

Ellie put down the bag of tapes she'd been holding. She stood for a moment, taking it in, and then she said quietly, 'Is his son alone in there?'

The nurse nodded. 'He said he wanted to be on his own for a while.'

'I understand that but I wonder if he might want to see me? I'd like to let him know I'm here.'

If he still wanted to be alone, she would leave, but she couldn't bear to think of him grieving and without comfort of any kind.

The nurse was doubtful, but after a bit more persuasion she reluctantly agreed, and Ellie went along the corridor to find the room. She knocked lightly on the door and waited.

'Ellie?' James pulled open the door. His face was ashen, his whole manner distracted, as if he was having trouble gathering his thoughts, and for a moment or two she wondered if she'd done the wrong thing in coming here. His gaze was blank. Perhaps he really did want to be alone.

Then he reached for her and she wrapped her arms around him, holding him tight as he told her what had happened. 'He had another heart attack yesterday evening,' he said in a taut voice. 'And after that he never recovered. He just… faded away…'

'I'm so sorry, James. I really thought he had a chance.'

He shook his head. 'I just never thought… I mean, I've been half expecting it for months, but now it's happened it feels all wrong. He should have been at home where I could care for him.'

'You did everything you could for him. No one could have done any more.' She gently stroked his back, soothing him as best she could. 'Anyway, he was frustrated by his illness. He was a strong man and even I guessed he hated being held back by his frailty. Perhaps he's at peace now.'

'Maybe. I hope so.'

He straightened up, and stepped out into the corridor, shutting the door behind him. 'I need to make some arrangements,' he said, but she shook her head.

'Not now, James. It will all wait. Let me take you home.'

He sighed. 'Okay. You're right, of course.' He gave a shuddery sigh. 'But I can drive myself home, and anyway you'll be needed in A and E.' He paused, trying to bring his chaotic thoughts under control. 'Why don't you come over to the house straight after work? I'd really appreciate it if you would do that.'

'All right. I'll be there.'

'Thanks, Ellie.'

She went out with him to the car park and watched him drive away. His expression was bleak, his eyes dark and empty, as though his emotions were all wrung out.

Somehow Ellie managed to get through the rest of her shift, though she had to force herself to concentrate.

'A few of the thyroid test results are back,' she told Olivia. 'I think we need to arrange for an endocrinologist to take a look at Jenny Soames.'

'I'll give Dr Mason a call,' Olivia suggested. 'Have you any idea what the treatment will be?'

'I imagine he'll put her on anti-thyroid medication, along with glucocorticoids. And of course he'll try to find out what caused the problem in the first place.'

'She's looking a bit better than she did earlier, anyway. She's cooler now and not quite so agitated.'

'That's good.'

Ellie handed over to the other registrar on duty a short time later and set off for the manor house. It had been heartbreaking to see James in such a sorry state that afternoon, and she could only hope that he might be feeling less battered by now.

'Hi,' he said, coming out to greet her when she parked her car on his drive some half an hour later. 'Come into the house.'

'Are you all right?' she asked him. 'How are you holding up?'

'I'm okay.' He led the way to the kitchen, where he pulled out a chair for her at the table before filling the kettle with water and switching it on. 'I'd rather not talk about what happened. I'd sooner keep busy, occupy my mind with something else. Does that sound bad?'

'No, not at all. It's probably understandable. It's hard for the mind to take in something like this.'

'You want tea or coffee, or maybe something stronger?'

'Tea will be fine, thanks.'

'Okay.' He put tea bags into the teapot and added boiling water. 'So, how did things go with your producer last night?'

'It wasn't too bad,' she answered. 'It was better than I expected, but I'm still not sure what's going to happen. It all depends on whether we can restore my image in the eyes of the public. After all, who wants to take advice from someone with a dubious background?'

'I think a lot of people will be able to identify with teenage rebellion,' he said quietly. 'I wanted to be there with you but...' His voice trailed away. 'I had a call from the hospital... and you know the rest.'

'Yes. I'm sorry.'

'I'd not long left there. He seemed to be recovering. He was cheerful and making plans for when he was to come home.' He shook himself, as though trying to clear his head. 'Have you had any more trouble with the press?'

'It's not been too bad. A couple of men were waiting outside for me this morning, but I told them I didn't have anything much to say. Except that I would always try to make good programmes and I wanted to help viewers understand more about their health and enable them to make wise decisions about their lifestyles.

'I said I would be sorry if all that came to an end because of some stories about my youthful indiscretions. And I told them there came a point when I'd realised I had to pull myself up from the downward spiral and stop seeing myself as a victim. I had to take responsibility for myself and make something of my life.'

'Good for you.'

She gave a rueful smile. 'Well, I decided I wasn't going to hide away any longer. I'm going to face up to whatever's out there.' She shrugged lightly, sloughing off the burden that had been weighing her down. 'Apparently I've had quite a lot of fan mail supporting me. That makes me feel a lot better.'

He poured tea and slid a cup towards her. 'Help yourself to milk and sugar.' He frowned. 'I ought to offer you something to eat. Come to think of it, I haven't had anything today.'

'You haven't eaten all day?'

He shook his head. 'I haven't felt like it. But I suppose...'

'What do you have?'

'I'm not sure. Harriet does most of the cooking. She's away at the moment, though, and won't be back for a few days. She's taking a holiday and she's gone to be with her daughter and her family in Wales.'

Ellie stood up. 'Do you mind if I have a look at what's in the cupboards?' She'd have to take over. It struck her that he wasn't in any state to make the simplest of decisions right now.

'No, go ahead.'

She had a look around and after a minute or two she said, 'I can make spaghetti Bolognese. How does that sound?'

'Fine. What can I do to help?'

They worked together, chopping onions, carrots and celery and then tossing these into a pan. Ellie added minced beef to the mix, cooking it for a while, and then added a broth along with a dash of red and white wine. She showed James how to make a sauce with tomatoes and herbs, and they left all of that to simmer for a while. Finally, James placed spaghetti in a pan of hot water, and within a few minutes the meal was ready to serve.

'I think I'd like to have you around all the time,' James murmured as they sat down to eat, and he wound spaghetti around his fork. 'This is the best spaghetti Bolognese I've ever tasted.'

'Oh, really! You just want me for my cooking abilities?'

James smiled. 'I can think of a few other reasons,' he said.

Ellie would have answered but her phone's ring tone sounded, and she gave him an apologetic look. 'Sorry, I should have turned it off.'

'No, don't do that. You should answer it. It might be important.'

She glanced at the caller display, and pulled a face. 'It's Ben, my producer.'

She answered the call, and discovered that Ben was in an upbeat mood. 'Something's happened that you'll never believe,' he said. 'I've had a call from your mother.'

'My *mother*?' Ellie echoed. 'Why would my mother be getting in touch with you?'

'Well, she read all the stuff about you in the papers, and she was worried about the effect it was having on the programme. Some of the articles were hinting that the series would be stopped and she was worried about that. It seems she follows your programme religiously.'

Ellie was surprised. 'I didn't know that.'

'Anyway, it seems she wants to put the record straight. I think she wanted me to know that none of this was your fault—actually, I knew that already—but she was calling to let me know she's going to the newspapers. She says she wants to tell her story—that it was because she left that you went off the rails.'

'But why didn't she tell me what she was planning?'

'She thought you might try to stop her. I think she's overwhelmed with guilt about the past and she wants to make it right. She's planning on giving you and Noah any proceeds from the articles, so she's certainly not doing it for the money.'

Ellie frowned. 'But she'll ruin her own life doing that. She mustn't. What will people think of her?'

'It's too late to do anything about it now. She'd already contacted the papers before she rang me. The article will be in the weekend issues. All of which makes me positive that we'll go ahead with the programmes we've planned and make a new series based on teenage problems. This is good news for you, Ellie.'

Ellie wasn't at all sure about that. Ben cut the call a short time later, and she stared into space for a minute or two.

'I put your plate in the oven to keep warm while you were talking on the phone,' James said. 'I'll get it for you.'

'That was thoughtful of you.' She gave him a quick smile. 'Thanks.'

He lifted her plate from the oven and slid it onto the table, looking at her in concern. 'Is everything all right?'

'It depends how you look at it.' She told him what Ben had said, breaking off to eat her spaghetti now and again. 'It's strange, but I feel as though I want to protect her. That's odd, isn't it?'

'Not really. She's your mother, after all. Whatever happens, whatever they do, our parents are a deep part of our psyche.'

She reached out and covered his hand with hers. 'Yes.'

He responded by gripping her hand warmly, and it was as though they had formed a bond, something that brought them together in their time of need.

They were still holding hands when there was a brief rapping sound and then the kitchen door opened. Ellie gazed in surprise as Sophie stepped into the room. She hadn't expected her to appear out of the blue like that, but then she remembered that James had told her she had a key so that she could come and go as she pleased.

Sophie glanced at them and said, 'I didn't realise that you had company. I came to see how you are, James. This must have been a terrible day for you.'

James nodded, and slowly released Ellie's hand. 'Yes.'

'Well, I'm here for you now. You don't have to worry about anything. I'll help you with all the arrangements. There will be a lot to do, I expect.'

He nodded, standing up to greet her. 'Would you like some wine?' he asked, waving a hand towards the opened bottle at the side of the table. 'I'll get another glass.'

'Thank you.'

Sophie sat down at the table. 'I see you've already eaten,' she said. 'I was going to suggest that we get in a takeaway, but obviously that's redundant now.' She smiled as James handed her a glass. 'You must let me organise things for you. I'll go with you to make the arrangements—you won't be in any shape to take it all in. I think we should go first thing tomorrow. And then I'll organise the flowers and so on.'

Ellie shifted uncomfortably. James couldn't handle any of this right now. He wanted some time to grieve, to get himself together, before he launched into all the preparations that were such an unhappy necessity. Ought she to say something to Sophie?

She tried to catch her eye to give her a warning look, but Sophie wasn't making any eye contact with her.

'White lilies would be best, don't you think? With perhaps some white carnations slipped in among them.'

James went over to the window and closed his eyes briefly, as though trying to shut himself off from what lay ahead. He opened his mouth to answer but no sound came out, and Ellie decided it was time to intervene.

'I don't think James is ready to make arrangements yet, Sophie. He's still in shock. Maybe it would be best if he had a bit more time to take in what's happened.'

'Oh, of course. You're right. I should have thought of that.' Sophie stood up and went to stand beside James, laying a hand affectionately on his arm. 'Like I said, I'm here for you. We'll just take it easy for a while. Do whatever you want to do.'

'I know you mean well, Sophie. Thanks for trying to help.' James smiled at her, and as they talked quietly Ellie began to feel like an intruder.

To cover her confusion, she set about clearing the table, stacking crockery in the dishwasher and wiping down work surfaces.

'I need to go and check on something,' James said after a while. 'Sophie's reminded me that there's a problem with the stove in the drawing room. I should sort it out if we want to go and sit in there.'

He and Sophie left the room, presumably to go to the drawing room, but Ellie went on with tidying up. She threw out some fading flowers and emptied the waste bin, putting in a fresh liner. Then she prepared the coffee machine to make a fresh brew.

Sophie came in as she was setting out a tray with cups and saucers. 'James is not saying much at all,' she said softly. 'He seems totally preoccupied. I think it's probably best if we leave him alone for a while. I don't think he's in the mood for company.'

Ellie frowned. 'I suppose that's understandable.'

'Anyway, I'll see to the coffee,' Sophie murmured, filling a jug with cream from the fridge and adding a bowl of brown sugar to the tray. 'I expect you'll want to get off home now. James will be fine with me. I'll take care of him.' She smiled. 'It is my role, after all.'

'Is it?'

'Of course.' Sophie seemed surprised by Ellie's lack of knowledge. 'James has been too busy for any kind of commitment up to now, but it's always been taken for granted that I'll be his wife one day. Now that his father's sadly no longer with us, he'll need me by his side so that he can take his place as the next Lord Birchenall. It's not really a situation for a single man. I expect we'll make it a spring wedding.'

Ellie swallowed carefully, trying to take it all in. If any of this was the truth, why had James been so attentive towards her?

'You must be wondering why James has been so involved with you lately,' Sophie said, guessing Ellie's thoughts with pinpoint accuracy. 'It doesn't mean anything. He's a kind and thoughtful man, and he wanted to look after you when you were in trouble. But being with you would never have led to anything, you know. He might have had his head turned for a while, but that would never last.'

She looked in the wall cupboard and drew out a packet of mint chocolate biscuits and shook some out onto a plate. 'You should know, it's ingrained in his very being that he must marry someone with an impeccable background, someone who can carry off the role of being his wife with perfect ease. He needs a woman who can organise his dinner parties, entertain guests from the highest levels of society. That's why he's always kept me by his side. He needs me...'

Ellie tried to breathe slowly and evenly, to keep herself as calm as possible. If Sophie was making this up, she was doing it with an unsurpassed expertise.

She said slowly, 'Doesn't it bother you that he might have been seeing another woman?'

'It's a flirtation, nothing more. It doesn't mean anything. Once we're married, all that will come to an end. James has far too much integrity to jeopardise his future standing. Perhaps he's been testing the water elsewhere, but I'm not worried about it. I know that it was just a fleeting thing while he struggled to come to terms with settling down.'

Sophie poured coffee into two cups. 'Anyway, I won't delay you any longer,' she said. 'I'm sure you have things to do. I'll take good care of James from now on. You don't need to worry about that—I had his father's blessing, after all.'

That, at least, was true. Ellie frowned, not

wanting to leave but conscious that James wasn't here, in the kitchen, asking her to stay. Perhaps Sophie was right in what she was saying.

'Goodbye, Ellie.' Sophie picked up the tray and started towards the door. 'Don't forget your jacket. It's turning chilly outside.'

Deeply troubled, Ellie stared at the door for a while after she'd gone. Sophie was so sure of herself, so accustomed to having the run of this place, that she made her feel like an outsider.

Slowly, she retrieved her jacket from the back of a chair. Maybe Sophie expected her to simply disappear from James's life, but she wasn't going to do that. And for the time being she would at least go and find James and say goodbye.

'It seems to be working well enough now,' he said, looking up from his inspection of the cast-iron stove as Ellie followed Sophie into the room.

He glanced at the tray Sophie was carrying and frowned. 'Only two cups?'

'I've just remembered there's something I must go and do,' Ellie said. 'So I'll say goodbye. If you need me at all, if you want any help with anything, just give me a call. Maybe I'll see you back at work when you've had some time to get yourself together. Don't rush things. You should take as long as you need.'

He went with her to the front door. 'I'd hoped you might stay,' he said, and she wanted to put her arms around him and hold him close.

Instead, she said quietly, 'I think Sophie's planning on staying with you.'

'Yes.'

She walked to her car, and then with one last look around she slid into the driver's seat and started the engine.

What Sophie had said made perfect sense. James had seen *her* as a pleasant diversion, but ultimately he would marry Sophie, just as his father had wished. Why would he risk tainting his family's aristocratic lineage by associating with a woman whose life story was being splashed all over the pages of a Sunday newspaper?

CHAPTER TEN

'IT'S REALLY GOOD to see you again.' Ellie drank in James's features as she walked with him towards the ambulance bay. She'd heard he was back at work, but she had been busy with patients and hadn't seen him all morning. Now, though, she was overwhelmed by her feelings for him.

He didn't respond as she'd hoped, though. She longed to see the warm, easygoing man she'd come to love, but it looked as though it wasn't to be.

Instead, he was tense, his dark eyes shuttered, and she wasn't sure if that was because he was still in mourning or... She hardly dared think about it. Could it be that he was putting up a barrier between them now that he had made up his mind to be with Sophie?

Then again, perhaps he was simply on edge because he was preparing to deal with an emergency patient. There had been a road traffic accident, and a young man was being brought into A and E.

She pulled in a deep breath. 'I missed you,' she said.

'Did you?'

She nodded. She'd missed him more than he could ever know. It had been heartbreaking to walk away from him that night, and over and over she'd kept asking herself if Sophie had been telling the truth. But wouldn't he have contacted her if he had wanted to see her again?

She said slowly, 'I thought the funeral went very well…if these things can ever be thought of that way. The service was lovely, and the flower arrangements were beautiful, especially those inside the church.' Her brows drew together. 'I suppose Sophie was responsible for that.'

'No. I wanted to deal with everything myself. I felt it was important that I should do that.'

Ellie sent him a quick, sharp glance. That revelation surprised her, given that Sophie had been so keen to have a hand in everything. But perhaps it was all deeply personal to him and he hadn't wanted anyone else making those decisions.

'I was hoping to see you afterwards,' she said, 'but you must have gone away straight after the funeral. Harriet told me you went to stay with relatives.'

'You came to the house?'

'Yes.' She lifted her shoulders. 'I realise now that I should have rung first. I expect Harriet forgot to mention it to you. She was a bit harassed at the time.' Her mouth made a rueful line. 'Sophie was there and I think she was trying to suggest a few changes to the menus Harriet was planning.'

He gave a wry smile, the first chink to show in his armour. 'That was probably a bad move. Once she's organised herself, Harriet hates any interference in the kitchen.'

'Yes, I guessed as much, though I've always

got on well with her. She was good to me when we lived at the lodge.'

They reached the ambulance bay and waited. A siren sounded in the distance and Ellie knew it would only be a minute or two before it arrived.

'I went away to spend some time with the family,' James said. 'Aunts and uncles...cousins. I needed to take some time out to clear my head and the hospital authorities granted me some compassionate leave. I'll make it up to them with overtime over the next few weeks.'

'I'm sure they won't expect you to do that,' she said with a frown. 'Everyone understands that you've just lost your father.'

'Maybe.'

The ambulance stopped in front of the doors to the emergency unit, and as soon as the paramedics had wheeled the injured man from the back of the vehicle, James hurried forward to meet him.

'His name's Sam Donnelly,' the paramedic said. 'He came off his motorbike. When we first found him he was trying to talk but we couldn't make out what he was saying. He's become much less responsive now, though, and his heart rate is very low.'

'Thanks.'

They left the paramedic to go back to his vehicle and hurried to the resuscitation room, where James immediately began his examination of the patient. 'Let's get him on a cardiac monitor.'

'I'll sort it.' Olivia went to set up the machine.

'His blood pressure's dropping,' Ellie warned him urgently. 'I'll put in an IV line and take some blood for cross-matching.' Sam looked to be about eighteen years old, and she couldn't help wondering how his parents must be feeling, left behind in the relatives' waiting room, knowing that their son was unconscious and that he might be dreadfully injured.

'Okay.' He started to insert an endotracheal tube into the young man's windpipe and then connected the oxygen supply.

He frowned as he went on with his examination. 'His condition's deteriorating by the minute,' he said. 'He's very pale, breathing rapidly, and his pulse is weak and thready.'

'His body temperature is low, too,' Ellie remarked. Sam's skin was moist and clammy and she was beginning to be very concerned about him. He must have been hurt badly in the accident for this to be happening, but apart from some gashes on his face, arms and legs there were no visible signs of any major injury that would have caused his collapse.

'Clearly, he's going into hypovolaemic shock but there's no obvious reason for the instability. We'd better put in a couple of wide-bore cannulas and give him fluids to compensate.' James was thoughtful as he continued to check over the young man. 'He must be bleeding internally, but we need to find out where it's coming from. And we need to find out quickly.'

'Do you want to do an ultrasound scan?'

He nodded. 'Hopefully, that will tell us what we want to know.' He glanced at Olivia, who was monitoring the patient's vital signs. 'Would you give Theatre a ring and tell them we might have a patient for them? They need to be prepared.'

'Okay.'

He set up the equipment and said cautiously, 'He probably has lower rib fractures so I think we should be looking for blunt abdominal trauma.'

'That sounds logical.'

The scan, though, wasn't particularly helpful, and James asked the nurse to get the equipment ready so that he could do a diagnostic peritoneal lavage.

Ellie helped him to prepare the patient, and James used a local anaesthetic as he made a small incision in Sam's abdomen, before carefully introducing a dialysis catheter into the peritoneal cavity. Then he flushed warm saline into the opening, before slowly aspirating it back into the transparent bag.

'There's a lot of blood in there,' Ellie observed with a frown, watching the saline slowly turn red. 'It could be that his liver was damaged by the broken ribs.'

'It looks that way. We'll send him up to Theatre right away for a laparotomy.' He turned to Olivia. 'Will you give them another call and make sure they're ready for him up there?'

'I will.'

Ellie prepped the young man for surgery. The sooner he was operated on, the better his chances of survival would be.

They watched as he was wheeled away to Theatre, and James took off his protective gloves and tossed them into the bin. 'You did well back there,' he said, glancing at Ellie. 'It's good to see that you have your confidence back.'

'I suppose that's true,' she said with a small frown. 'I didn't even think about what I was doing. It was instinctive. And yet…'

'And yet?'

She pulled a face. 'Earlier today I had some news that knocked me back a bit. Olivia told me she'd had a call from Mel this morning. She wants to come in and see me.' Normally, that would have been enough to put her off her stroke, but perhaps with James returning to work she'd had other things to think about.

'Did she say why?'

'No. But I agreed to the meeting.' She looked at her watch. 'She'll be here soon, in about fifteen minutes.'

'Do you want me to be there with you?'

She smiled with relief. 'Would you? I'm really not looking forward to seeing her. What if she was the one who went to the tabloids with the stories about me? She knew me well enough back then after all, and she does have a grudge against me.'

'We'll try to find out.' He looked at her, taking in the green scrubs and soft plastic overshoes she was wearing. 'Maybe we should get ready to meet her?'

She nodded. She wasn't exactly sure of the reason, but her spirits had lifted as soon as he'd offered to stay with her. He'd seemed like a stranger to her at first today but now he was back, the man she loved more than any other, and no matter how much her head warned her to be cautious, it was being firmly overruled by her heart.

'We'll see her in my office,' James said, when they met up again, dressed in normal, everyday clothes.

She nodded and went with him, and almost as soon as they had entered the room, Mel knocked on the door.

'Won't you take a seat?' James invited her with a reassuring smile. 'I've just made coffee, so perhaps we should get comfortable and then you can tell us what the problem is?'

'It's not a problem,' Mel said. 'It's more about a decision I've made.' She was dressed in a businesslike fashion, as before, but her hair was styled more freely this time, with a slight wave to soften her appearance. She wore a dress with a matching three-quarter-length jacket.

She sipped the coffee James gave her and seemed to be taking a moment to gather her thoughts.

'A decision?' Ellie prompted her.

Mel took a deep breath. 'I was very upset when my aunt died. I was angry and frustrated, because everything happened so quickly. One day she was talking to me, making plans to come with me on a weekend trip to the seaside, and within a few more days she had died. I couldn't take it in. She was like a mother to me, and I loved her.'

She reached for her coffee with a trembling hand and hesitated, as though she couldn't go on.

'Take your time,' James said. 'We know this is difficult for you.'

She nodded. 'I've been to see a lawyer,' she said at last.

Ellie's heart lurched, and a wave of nausea rose in her as her stomach clenched involuntarily. She could see her career, everything she'd worked for, beginning to dissolve. Sitting across the table from her, James's gaze caught hers. He knew exactly what she was going through.

'He looked into the hospital records,' Mel went on. 'He talked to an expert about my aunt's illness, and found out that there was an operation that could have been done, where a kind of window is made in the tissue around the heart to re-move the infected matter.'

'That's true,' Ellie told her. 'It's usually done if the illness is chronic and drainage hasn't been successful. In your aunt's case, the infection was overwhelming and didn't respond to the antibi-otics, but it was the fact that her heart was weak that was the biggest problem. Her heart stopped. She went into cardiac arrest, and I did everything I could for her, but unfortunately she wasn't able to respond to the treatment. I'm sorry.'

'I know.' Mel grimaced. 'I understand now. I think perhaps I didn't want to see it before. I was devastated when my aunt passed away and I wanted someone to blame.' She looked at Ellie. 'I'm sorry I put you through all that. I know it wasn't your fault.'

Ellie exhaled slowly. 'Thank you for coming to tell me.'

'I saw the stories that were published about you,' Mel said. She shook her head. 'I thought it was really unfair. I remembered some of those times, the parties, the rowdiness. We were to-gether a lot of the time, and you were never bad. You always wanted to help people, even though you were upset about what was going on at home. I hope your mother's account has helped to put things right.'

'You saw the article?'

Mel nodded. 'At least she realised that she was partly to blame. Perhaps, at the time, she didn't understand what pain she was causing, but the truth seems to have come home to her now.'

'I think we've both gone some way to freeing ourselves from the past. She helped a lot by explaining what had gone on, and it must have taken a lot of courage for her to do that. It made me feel better about her.' She smiled. 'We met up and talked and brought things out into the open, so at least we have some sort of understanding of one another now.'

They talked for a while longer, and then Ellie went with her to the door. 'Goodbye, Mel,' she said. 'Thanks again for coming to see me.'

She went back into the office and closed the door, resting her spine against it for a moment as she absorbed everything that had happened. She hadn't expected Mel to look at things from another angle, and it was a huge relief to know that she had withdrawn the complaint.

As to her mother, it had been good to see her again and have the chance to talk things through.

'I've wanted to do this for a long time,' her mother had said. 'I wanted to see you and try to put things right, but I wasn't sure how you would feel about seeing me.'

'I'm glad we've found each other again,' Ellie had told her. 'I feel as though a huge burden has been lifted from me. I know it took a lot for you to open up to the press like that, and I realise, now, that you had been ill for a long time. We were wrong to blame you.'

'Thank you for that.' Her mother had smiled. 'I didn't want to let you go. You and Noah were so young, but I didn't have the strength to go on. I'm better now, though, and I hope we can make up for everything that's happened.'

'We can. We will. We'll start afresh from here, Mum.'

She came out of her reverie and became aware that James was watching her.

'Are you okay?' he asked, and she nodded.

'I'm fine. Everything's good.'

'I'm glad.' His gaze was thoughtful. 'But we are left with a small puzzle to solve. If Mel didn't go to the press and start all the hoo-hah,' he said quietly, 'who did?'

'I don't know.' She frowned. She was beginning to have a shrewd idea who might have been behind it, but she was going to keep that to herself for now. There was only one person who might have reason to sully her reputation after all, but James was close to Sophie and she wasn't going to accuse anyone without proof.

He came over to her. 'Anyway, I'm glad all that business is over. You can get on with your life now without any worries.'

'Yes. It's a huge relief. Thanks for standing by me.'

'I told you once before, I'll always be there for you, Ellie.' He looked at her steadily. 'You can rely on me.'

If only she could believe that. But he was going to be with Sophie, wasn't he?

'That's a comforting thought,' she said, moving away from the door, 'but you didn't seem too thrilled to be with me earlier. You were very tense, but perhaps there were things on your mind?'

His dark brows drew together. 'Maybe I *was* a bit preoccupied. The last time I saw you, you walked out on me. I'd been hoping you might stay over at the house. I wanted to be with you. But you left, and you didn't call the next day. I couldn't think why you would suddenly pull back from me, except you might have decided it was a bad idea to be involved with me.'

'No.' She sent him a quick, insistent glance. 'It was nothing like that. Sophie told me that you and she were getting together, that you were going to be married.'

'What?' It was an explosive sound. 'Good grief, how did she manage to come up with that idea?'

Ellie was confused. 'But you've been together for a long time—your father told me she was right for you, and he gave me the impression you would be marrying her.'

'My father had lots of ideas about how things should go, but we didn't always agree. And I certainly wouldn't do something simply because it was what he wanted. I loved him and respected him, but we're different people and I have my own way of going about things.' He frowned as someone knocked on the door. 'Not now,' he muttered under his breath.

Olivia came into the room. 'Sam Donnelly's back from Theatre,' she said. 'His liver and spleen were ruptured, but the surgeon was able to repair the damage. I thought you might want to come and check on him.'

'Thanks, Olivia.'

She left the room and he turned back to face Ellie. 'I need to go and see him. Look, Ellie, I'm going to talk to Sophie and get this sorted out. I'll come and see you this evening, as soon as I'm done.'

'All right.' What was she to make of all this? From the sound of things, Sophie had been making it up as she'd gone along…because she wanted Ellie out of the way? Well, she'd succeeded in that, hadn't she?

But James had been disappointed that she hadn't stayed with him. That was what had her heart singing. That was what sent her hopes soaring skywards. Was there a chance for them after all?

She went with him to see how Sam was doing, and felt reassured that his blood pressure and heart rate were improving. It would take him some time to heal and recover, but thankfully his life was no longer in danger.

She went home at the end of her shift, and stopped to say hello to her neighbour, Lily, who was just coming back from the shops with the baby and Jayden.

'Hi, there. How are things going?' Ellie chatted to Lily and admired Jayden's toy car, and peeped into the buggy to coo over the gorgeous new addition to the family. 'Hello, Amy. Aren't you a tiny little thing?' The only answer she received was a sleepy yawn and a delicate sucking sound as the baby pursed her pink rosebud mouth and went back to dreaming of creamy milk.

Both women chuckled, and after a while Ellie left to go and make herself look presentable for when James arrived. She wasn't sure what to expect. Would Sophie persuade him that she was only going on what he'd led her to believe over the last few years?

She made herself a snack and then went upstairs to shower and change into jeans and a pretty camisole top. She put on a light smattering of make-up, adding a pale bronze blusher to lend colour to her cheeks, and left her hair loose. Then, feeling a bit more sure of herself, she went downstairs to wait for James.

He turned up soon after, and she opened the door to him cautiously, not knowing what to expect.

'I wasn't sure whether you would already have eaten,' he said in a quizzical tone.

'Just a snack,' she told him. 'A couple of crackers and cheese. Why?'

He produced a white plastic carrier bag that he'd been hiding behind his back. 'I brought Chinese food. I'm starving, so I'm hoping you're ready for this, too.'

'I love Chinese food,' she said, sliding plates into the oven to warm and breathing in the wonderful aroma. He slid the packages onto the kitchen table and she drooled over the contents. 'Beef with green peppers in black bean sauce, special fried rice, sweet and sour chicken... Oh, I'm in heaven...'

He laughed. 'I'll put the kettle on. Unless you want wine? I can go and get a bottle.'

'That's all right, I have wine in the fridge.' She went to get it, while James took cutlery from a drawer and set the table.

They sat down to eat and she tasted the sweetly battered chicken, following it up with a forkful of rice. 'This is delicious. Yum.'

He smiled as he speared a prawn with his fork. 'Yes, it is.'

They chatted about this and that, and finally she finished her meal and put down her fork.

'I wish I had more room in my stomach,' she said woefully. 'It's my favourite, and I can't do it justice.'

He laughed. 'I'll bring you some more, whenever you want.'

'So you'll be coming back?'

'Do you think you could keep me away?'

'I wouldn't want to.'

'That's good. That's what I really want to hear.'

She absorbed that with a smile of contentment, leaning back in her seat. 'Shall we take the wine and finish it off in the living room?'

'That sounds like a good idea.'

He went with her and poured more wine before coming to sit beside her on the sofa. Watching him, long and lithe and gorgeous, she was wistful and her expression became serious.

'Did you go and see Sophie?'

'I did.' He frowned.

'So, what happened?'

'She confessed that she'd lied to you. She also admitted to leaking the stories about you to the tabloids.'

'I thought she might have been behind it.' She was puzzled, though. 'But how did she know about me when I was a teenager?'

'She quizzed my father about your family being at the lodge and what happened after you left. He told her about the newspaper articles, so she passed that information on to the papers.'

She was still for a moment, taking it in, and then pulled herself together. 'She must have been very insecure,' she said.

He nodded. 'I'm sure she was.'

'So you never intended to marry her?'

'I didn't ever have a relationship with her, apart from a couple of dinner invitations with friends, never mind want to marry her. She just let it be known to anyone who would listen that she and I were together. I think that's where your brother came by the idea that we were a couple.

'I warned her that I didn't share her feelings,' he went on, 'but she didn't listen. Perhaps she thought I would change my mind. Either way, she must have been living in a fantasy world and it didn't help that she managed to work her way into my father's affections. She was always there for him.'

He thought about that for a moment. 'To be fair, she looked after him really well, making sure he had his medication, driving him around when he couldn't manage it himself and I wasn't available. But I think, all the time, she was working on the idea that we would be an item.'

'I almost feel sorry for her.'

He nodded. 'Of course, when you came along, she must have seen you as a threat. Anyone with half an eye could see that I'd fallen for you.'

'Had you?' She sent him a quick glance, her heart beginning to thump heavily. 'I don't know about that. I wasn't sure what you really felt for me. I mean, I know you wanted me, but you said you weren't ready for commitment and I started to realise that I didn't want to settle for anything less.'

His grey eyes homed in on her face. 'Are you saying you wanted to be with me?'

'Yes, I did. I do. But your father had such expectations for you. I felt as though my name had been tarnished, and he would never accept someone like me being involved with you.'

He gave her a rueful smile. 'It wasn't his decision to make. Anyway, after he got to know you better, and especially after you saved his life, he thought of you with affection. He told me he wished he could make it up to you and your family for the way he'd treated your father.'

'I'm pleased about that.'

He wrapped his arms around her, making her feel cosseted and cherished. 'I should never have doubted you,' he said. 'But I was afraid Lewis might persuade you he needed you, and somehow turn your head, and even though I knew you weren't the kind of person who would break up a marriage, I was consumed by this insane jealousy every time I saw you with him. It was total madness. I know Lewis would never do anything to hurt Jessica.' He frowned. 'Perhaps it was because I wasn't sure of your feelings.'

'I was just as guilty,' she said softly. 'I kept thinking you were dating Sophie at the same time that you were seeing me. I should have had more faith in you.'

'I don't want any other woman, Ellie. Only you.' He kissed her tenderly, his hands stroking her and bringing her closer to him.

'Is it really true?' She was desperate to believe him. 'You said you didn't want commitment and I was so afraid I was falling for you. I knew I would be devastated if you didn't feel the same way I did.'

'It's true, believe me. I never thought it would happen to me, but when we spent that time together on the boat I realised that I wanted to be with you all the time. It hit me hard, like a thunderbolt. I'm only really happy when I'm with you. I feel as though I'm at peace with the world and myself.' He kissed her again. 'It's as though I've found my soul mate. I love you.'

'Oh, James, I love you so much. I didn't know it could be like this.' She lifted her arms and let her fingers trail through the silky hair at the back of his head. 'I've been longing to hear you say you feel the same way, too.'

She kissed him lovingly, thrilled by the way his body meshed with hers, as though he couldn't get enough of her. With every part of her being, she yearned for him.

'Ellie, will you marry me?' he said huskily. 'I need to know that you'll be with me through everything, for all time.'

'Oh, yes, James.' She smiled up at him, her lips parting for his kiss. 'Yes, please. It's what I want, more than anything.' She sighed happily, losing herself in his arms, clinging to him as they kissed fiercely, passionately, with all the love and longing that spilled over into that wonderful, satisfying embrace. Like he'd said, they would be together for all time, she knew it.

* * * * *

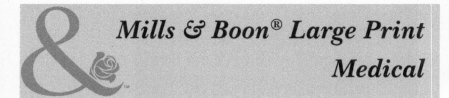

Mills & Boon® Large Print

Medical

April

May

June

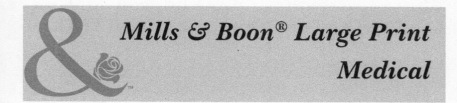

Mills & Boon® Large Print

Medical

July

HER HARD TO RESIST HUSBAND	Tina Beckett
THE REBEL DOC WHO STOLE HER HEART	Susan Carlisle
FROM DUTY TO DADDY	Sue MacKay
CHANGED BY HIS SON'S SMILE	Robin Gianna
MR RIGHT ALL ALONG	Jennifer Taylor
HER MIRACLE TWINS	Margaret Barker

August

TEMPTED BY DR MORALES	Carol Marinelli
THE ACCIDENTAL ROMEO	Carol Marinelli
THE HONOURABLE ARMY DOC	Emily Forbes
A DOCTOR TO REMEMBER	Joanna Neil
MELTING THE ICE QUEEN'S HEART	Amy Ruttan
RESISTING HER EX'S TOUCH	Amber McKenzie

September

WAVES OF TEMPTATION	Marion Lennox
RISK OF A LIFETIME	Caroline Anderson
TO PLAY WITH FIRE	Tina Beckett
THE DANGERS OF DATING DR CARVALHO	Tina Beckett
UNCOVERING HER SECRETS	Amalie Berlin
UNLOCKING THE DOCTOR'S HEART	Susanne Hampton

Discover more romance at

www.millsandboon.co.uk

- ❤ WIN great prizes in our exclusive competitions
- ❤ BUY new titles before they hit the shops
- ❤ BROWSE new books and REVIEW your favourites
- ❤ SAVE on new books with the Mills & Boon® Bookclub™
- ❤ DISCOVER new authors

PLUS, to chat about your favourite reads, get the latest news and find special offers:

- 🔲 Find us on facebook.com/millsandboon
- 🐦 Follow us on twitter.com/millsandboonuk
- ❤ Sign up to our newsletter at millsandboon.co.uk